Fernando's Gold

TOM PARRY

A Black Horse Western

ROBERT HALE · LONDON

© Tom Parry 2003
First published in Great Britain 2003

ISBN 0 7090 7326 7

Robert Hale Limited
Clerkenwell House
Clerkenwell Green
London EC1R 0HT

Typeset by
Derek Doyle & Associates, Liverpool.
Printed and bound in Great Britain by
Antony Rowe Limited, Wiltshire

For Mrs Beryl May
who gave me the original idea

CHAPTER 1

Scarne watched the five men riding up to his shack with growing unease. He had been around long enough to spot trouble when he saw it. And the five men spelled trouble with a capital T.

Scarne stepped out into the open in front of the shack. He held a Winchester at the ready.

'All right, that's far enough,' he shouted.

The five men reined in their horses. Whether they were surprised or not to see a man with a gun who had the obvious intention of using it, it didn't show on their faces.

Their leader, the one who was riding the white stallion answered. 'We only want some water for ourselves and the horses. We've been riding for days and we're thirsty.'

Scarne studied them. They looked like outlaws. They had the hard faces of men who were used to killing and who wouldn't think twice about it. He was an outlaw himself. It takes one to recognize one, he thought mirthlessly.

As he watched them one of the five began to move his horse surreptitiously. He began to inch his way to the left of the group. The only reason for doing so was the obvious one of trying to get round to the back of the shack. From there he would be able to take Scarne in a crossfire if necessary.

'Well, are you going to let us have water or not?' demanded the leader, irritably. Although he spoke with a Texan drawl he wasn't a typical Texan. He was short and stocky. Scarne was still watching the fifth member of the party out of the corner of his eye. He had now moved about twenty yards from the other four. Although in the beginning his movements had been almost imperceptible, now they had become more definite. The rider, a weather-beaten thin man with his Stetson pulled down over his forehead, had his gaze firmly fixed on the corner of the shack for which he was heading.

Suddenly the scene changed. The girl came out of the shack behind Scarne. He had called her a girl since the time of their first meeting, although she claimed to be twenty years old. Whether she was lying he had never been interested in finding out. She had arrived at the shack one evening in a distressed state, having claimed that the wagon in which she had been travelling with her father had been attacked by Apaches. He had taken her in.

The following day he had set out with her to find the spot where she said the Apaches had attacked the wagon and shot her father. She claimed she had only managed to escape because a sandstorm had blown up and the Apaches hadn't been able to spot her.

They hadn't been able to find the wagon. Because of the sandstorm they also hadn't been able to find any traces of the Indians. Scarne wasn't sure whether he believed her story or not. Anyhow it didn't matter. He had taken her in. At first she had been merely a housekeeper. Then later, without any bidding from Scarne, she had come to his bed. He guessed that one day she would disappear as suddenly as she had arrived. Then he would be able to go back to his uncomplicated bachelor existence. Because there was no doubt that females complicated things. Exactly as the girl was doing now.

'Tell your husband we just want some water, then we'll leave,' stated the leader.

'He's not my husband,' retorted the girl.

She was wearing the skimpy white spotted dress that she had worn when she had turned up at the shack. She had stated that all her clothes were in a trunk which the Apaches had seized. She had added that they had pulled the clothes out of the trunk and were trying them on and whooping with delight when she had made her escape. Whether by intention or not the dress was the sort that

9

could inflame men's passions. It was obvious that it was having that effect on at least two of the outlaws, who were eyeing her lasciviously.

'Let them have the water, Scarne,' she pleaded.

'So your name's Scarne,' said the leader. He seemed pleased that he had discovered some useful information.

The outlaw who had been heading for the corner of the shack had almost reached it. Scarne didn't hesitate. He aimed his Winchester and fired. The sound of the shot bounced off the nearby hills. Before any of the outlaws could draw their guns Scarne was again covering them with his Winchester.

'You've shot his horse,' shrieked the girl.

Which was exactly what he had done. He had shot the horse from under the outlaw who had been trying to reach the corner of the shack. The outlaw had jumped off in time.

'You bastard,' he yelled, as he hobbled back to join the others.

'You should have stayed with them,' said Scarne. 'You had no business sneaking round the back of the shack.'

Their leader took charge. 'You jump up behind Lewis,' he snapped. After the outlaw had obeyed, he turned to Scarne. 'We'll get you for this,' he snarled. 'We know you now. And we know your name.'

He turned his horse. The others followed suit.

As they rode away they fired their guns into the air. It was only an idle gesture. But somehow Scarne knew that their leader's words hadn't been an idle threat.

CHAPTER 2

The following day Scarne took the girl into Sula. She had claimed that she was worried that the bandits would return and seek their revenge for his shooting one of their horses.

He had agreed to take her into Sula. Truth to tell he wasn't too unhappy at the idea of getting rid of her. She was an uncommunicative little thing and any efforts he made at starting a conversation would usually be met with monosyllables. In the end he had given up trying to have any conversation with her. They had gone their separate ways in the shack and, except at mealtimes and bedtimes there had been no communication between them.

The meals she had cooked had been basic. Usually they were either soup or beans. Once he had asked her if she knew how to make tortillas – one of his favourite dishes. She had replied that she didn't know how to cook them. And that had been the end of trying to extend her culinary powers.

True, she had come to his bed. Probably in the first place because it was warmer than being curled up on the sofa. Their love-making had been without any passion on her part. After the first few weeks, and after being unable to elicit any spark of response, he had given up making love to her. It had been the end of any further physical contact between them.

They rode in silence for the thirteen or so miles to Sula. She clung closely to him on his horse. He had asked her what she intended doing when they reached Sula. She had replied that she intended trying to get employment in the theatre.

He had been surprised at the answer. 'What do you intend doing in the theatre?' he had asked.

'Anything,' she had replied. 'I can sing and dance. If I can't get a job on the stage I'm willing to help backstage.'

For the first time there was animation in her voice. Scarne stared at her, surprised.

'Have you worked in the theatre before?' he demanded.

'Yes. I ran away from home when I was thirteen. My mother used to beat me. In the end I had had enough. I ran away.'

Why couldn't she have revealed her past to him during the lonely evenings they had shared in the shack, thought Scarne. At least it would have helped to pass the time away.

'I went to a town named Hawkesville. There was a theatre there. They gave me a job taking the tickets. I loved it there. I stayed for three years. They used to put on plays and I used to have small parts. When I walked on the stage it was as if I was coming to life.'

Well there certainly hasn't been much life in you since, Scarne observed to himself.

Once the flood-doors were open she wouldn't stop talking. 'We used to have travelling companies, some would put on plays and others what they used to call vaudeville. They never had enough actors, they would usually give me a small part. Sometimes they would even give me a big one. I even played Cordelia in one of the productions of *King Lear.*'

'So why did you leave it?' demanded Scarne.

'Someone set fire to the theatre,' she replied, bitterly. 'They say it was a group of evangelists. They claimed that life in the theatre was like Sodom and Gomorrah.'

'And was it?' demanded an interested Scarne.

'Certainly not,' she replied, indignantly. 'I was a virgin until I met you.'

'I didn't know . . .' For the first time he was at a loss for words.'

'It didn't matter. It was just my way for paying you for taking me in during these past few months,' she said, dismissively.

They finally reached Sula. They rode down the

main street. A few women who were out shopping watched them interestedly. They saw a tall man in the saddle. That itself was not usual since most Texans were tall. He had an interesting rather than a handsome face. Somehow he looked the sort of man it wouldn't pay to cross. The girl in the saddle behind him was a skinny, pale-faced young creature. If she was staying in Sula she didn't look the type who would cause their husbands to turn their heads and regard her admiringly.

Scarne drew up outside the theatre which bore the name the Grand Theatre. They dismounted.

'I suppose this is the place,' he demanded.

'Oh, yes,' she said, excitedly.

In Scarne's eyes it looked a rather run-down establishment. It could certainly do with a coat of paint. In fact several.

The girl was holding out her hand. 'Well, good-bye, Scarne,' she said.

How do you say goodbye to someone who had been sharing your shack for the past six months and your bed for much of that time? He stared at her. She suddenly seemed more self-possessed, as if being near the theatre had suddenly given her a new confidence.

'Are you sure you'll be all right?' he asked, awkwardly.

'I'm bound to find a job here,' she replied. She was still holding out her hand.

16

Scarne took her tiny hand in his. He hadn't expected to feel any emotion at their leave-taking. To his surprise he felt rather sad.

'Good-bye, Victoria,' he said. He hadn't often used her name and to use it now seemed strange.

They shook hands formally. As she was about to turn and leave Scarne thrust a few notes into her hand. 'This will help to keep you going until you find something.'

She stared at him with pale-blue eyes as though seeing him for the first time. 'Thank you,' she said. She stood on tiptoe and kissed him on the lips. 'If you come into Sula again, come and see one of the shows. I'll be sure to be in it.' It was her parting shot as she turned and went into the theatre.

Scarne rode back to the shack. He had considered going to a saloon and having a meal and a perhaps a drink or two. But he had rejected the idea. He wanted to get back to the shack before nightfall.

When he was about half a mile away he suddenly realized that he was too late. There were the tell-tale signs of smoke in the air. It was straight ahead. On the exact spot where his shack would have been.

When he approached it he saw that it had been completely burned down. The chicken-house, too, had been burned down. The mutilated bodies of the chickens told him what the bandits had done with the hens they hadn't taken with them.

Incongruously only the stone pigsty survived. But if he had expected to find Rachel or one of her litter alive in it, he was mistaken. They had all been used as target practice by the outlaws.

The acre or so of garden in which Scarne had grown enough vegetables for their daily needs had been ridden over again and again until there was nothing edible left to be picked. The final straw was when he went round the back of the smouldering embers and saw another body. It was Daisy the cow, who had been shot.

At that moment Scarne decided to become a bounty hunter.

CHAPTER 3

Scarne collected some of the smouldering timber and used it to light a bonfire. He found one of the hens which hadn't been completely mutilated. He plucked it and roasted it on the bonfire. He added a few potatoes which the outlaws hadn't trampled on. It was to be his last dinner at the shack.

As he was eating it he reflected on the past couple of years which he had spent there. When he had arrived, travel-weary, he had been greeted with the same suspicion by its owner with which he had regarded the five outlaws yesterday. The owner had been a white-haired grizzled old man named Larsen. He had told Scarne that he would give him a warm meal and after that he could move on, otherwise he would shoot him.

It was obvious while they were eating their meal that Larsen was a sick man. He tried to conceal the fact from Scarne, but he didn't succeed in hiding it. After the meal Scarne told him that he would like to repay his kindness. He would chop up some of the timber for him. The winter was drawing near and the cold nights would soon be upon them.

Larsen made a feeble attempt to refuse to allow his visitor to chop up the timber, but Scarne ignored him. He went to the stand of willow trees at the side of the house and began to chop one of them down. Larsen watched him from an old armchair which stood outside the front of the house.

When Scarne had finished Larsen asked him: 'Would you like to stay here, son? All food found in exchange for running the place.'

'You've got a deal,' Scarne replied.

It was soon obvious that Larsen was very ill. In spite of the old man's protests that he didn't want anything to do with any quack doctor, Scarne fetched a doctor from Sula. The doctor diagnosed cancer and gave Larsen only three months to live. He survived for six. Scarne nursed him. In Larsen's final words he had expressed his gratitude. He added that he had left the shack to Scarne. It was all legal. There was a copy of the will in the tin trunk which he kept in his bedroom.

When Larsen died, Scarne went into Sula and notified the sheriff. He also checked with the lawyer that he was indeed the legal owner of the shack. Then he went to a saloon and got roaring drunk. He got so drunk that he took umbrage at the way three men at a nearby table were looking at him. The result was that he went over to them and asked them if there was anything wrong with his face.

They seemed highly amused by Scarne's question. Until he took the smaller of the three by his shirt collar and lifted him clear of his chair. This started a commotion. One against three wasn't very good odds for Scarne, although he succeeded in laying two of them out before the third one cracked him on the head with his revolver.

When Scarne came to the following morning he was lying on a straw mattress in a prison cell. His head felt as though it shouldn't be moved in case it fell off.

Eventually the sheriff came in. He was a middle-aged man with a sympathetic face. He had seen it all before. He told Scarne that he wouldn't have to go before the judge. In fact he could go home now.

Scarne mumbled his thanks. He had returned to the shack. There he had survived happily on his own – until the girl had arrived. Now she had gone and the shack had been destroyed. Scarne tossed the remains of a chicken bone into the fire. There was no point in dwelling on the past. He had an hour or so of daylight left to find out in which direction the outlaws had gone.

He searched around for their horses' tracks. It took him some time to find them. When he did discover them he gazed at them with relief.

The outlaws had headed west. That meant that the first town they would come across would be Hawkesville. It was about twenty miles away. It was a growing town. The sort of town where five outlaws would think they would be reasonably safe from the law. But not from a bounty hunter. He savoured the thought with satisfaction.

That night he spent in the only part of the shack that still had a roof – the pigsty.

CHAPTER 4

The following morning as Scarne rode towards Hawkesville a niggling thought kept recurring. There were five bandits and only one of him. The odds therefore were well and truly stacked in favour of the bandits.

One other thought in the cold light of reason hit him. Suppose in fact the bandits weren't wanted by the law. Suppose so far they had evaded having their names put up in the sheriffs' offices across the county as wanted men. That would mean he could be hunting them down without any recompense at the end of the day. And if you added to that the possibility that he would probably be shot in the process, since there were five of them and only one of him, his future prospects didn't appear to be too rosy.

These depressing thoughts almost made him change his mind and ride back to the ranch. But what if he did? What was there for him? He would have to start building up the shack again. Well, that wouldn't be too difficult. He was reasonably useful with his hands. He could afford to buy a cow, some hens and a pig. But it would take him several months to plant the vegetables and he knew that his heart wouldn't be in it. Having seen the shack burnt to the ground had somehow convinced him that he had reached the end of the line as a small-time farmer. It wasn't his kind of occupation. He had only stayed in the first place to look after Larsen. Then afterwards, when he had inherited the shack, it had seemed the obvious thing to do, to keep the farm going.

During the following months he had often thought about leaving the shack. It was a full-time day-and-night job running the farm. It wasn't his kind of work. He was a miner who had worked in a gold-mine over the border. It had been hazardous, but rewarding work. Yes, he had enjoyed working in the mine. He had enjoyed the company of the other miners. That was another disadvantage about the shack – it had been too lonely.

Not that he was the sort of person who went down to the saloon every evening. But he liked to join in with convivial company now and again. And living in the shack had definitely put an end to any prospect of social life. For a while he had thought that the arrival of the girl would provide an interesting and entertaining interlude. But her uncom-

municativeness had finally dashed any expecta-
tions he had harboured in that direction.

His thoughts were interrupted when he spotted
some riders on the horizon. He was too far away to
identify them. Also it was impossible to see in
which direction they were riding. He didn't take
any chances. He pulled his Winchester from its
sheath and began to thumb bullets into it.

As he rode further he could see that the riders
were in fact coming towards him. One other fact
which became apparent was that they were
Indians. Probably Apaches, since they were the
most common Indians in the area.

When they came within a couple of hundred
yards of him the leader raised his hand and they
stopped at his signal. Scarne counted five of them.
All danger comes in fives, he thought mirthlessly,
as he shifted the rifle. He was now holding the
reins of his horse with his left hand and holding
the rifle at the ready with his right.

Scarne's gaze was firmly fixed on the leader. At
that moment both his hands were fixed on the
horse's reins. But Scarne knew that Apaches
moved with deceptive rapidity. In a couple of
seconds the leader could draw the Colt which
Scarne had spotted hanging from his belt.

Scarne knew that the worst thing he could do
was to show the Apaches any fear. If they realized
that he was going to panic in the face of their presence, then he could be lost. His only course of

action was to ride straight ahead, even though it meant him coming within about twenty yards of them.

He kept his eyes firmly on them as he approached. They were young men. This made the situation more dangerous, since a young Apache was usually an Indian with something to prove. They sat still on their horses as he approached. As far as he could make out only the leader was carrying a gun. He had calculated that he would pass them on their left which would mean that he would be able to cover the leader with his Winchester as he rode by.

Of course the ultimate danger would be when he would have his back to them. He would be completely exposed to any bullets which the leader decided to aim at him.

The Indians were slightly spaced out. This gave Scarne a chance to check his original impression, that only their leader was carrying a gun. The others, though, would possess deadly throwing-knives, which could be just as effective as their leader's revolver.

He was now about fifty yards away. He knew it was now or never. He raised his rifle and pointed it at the leader.

'Go!' he shouted.

They showed no signs of obeying him. He could detect no expression on their faces. He stared at the leader. He had drawn up his horse and so he was now facing the leader. The Apache was bare to the waist. The only article of clothing above his waist was a silk scarf which was tied around the Apache's neck. It was a pink scarf with white spots. It was a woman's scarf. Scarne's thoughts flew to the story Victoria had told him about the Apaches who had attacked their wagon.

The Apache's hand moved like lightning towards his revolver. But Scarne's reaction was quicker. He brought his Winchester up and fired in the same movement.

Scarne's bullet hit the Apache. It didn't topple him from his horse though. The Apache struggled to stay on the horse's back. Scarne didn't hesitate. He pumped a couple more bullets into him. This time the Apache did fall from his horse. Scarne swung round quickly to cover the other Indians with his rifle. But they had already turned tail and were riding away as fast as they could.

Scarne dismounted. He confirmed that the Indian was indeed dead. He noticed that the revolver which the Indian had been hoping to use was lying in the sand. He went over and picked it up. It was an ordinary Colt which didn't appear to have been too well maintained. The paintwork was worn and the handle was chipped. However it was the initials which somebody had scratched on the handle which held his interest. He could make out the letters CF.

What had Victoria said was her surname? He

racked his brains for a few moments. Then it came to him. Foster. Yes, that was it. Victoria Foster.

So it looked as though her story about being ambushed by the Indians and her father being killed by them had been correct. He had only half-believed her when she had recounted it to him. The fact that they had not been able to find any evidence of the wagon nor of her father's body had not helped him to give any more credence to her story. But now he had found what was presumably her father's Colt. Added to which the scarf the Indian had been wearing almost definitely came from their wagon, putting her story in a new light.

In fact it was probably his recognition of the scarf on the Indian as belonging to a woman which gave him that split-second advantage over the Apache. It probably saved his life. Sometimes it's strange the way things work, he reflected, as he put the Colt revolver into his belt.

CHAPTER 5

Several hours later Scarne rode into Hawkesville. He had only visited the town once before when he had ridden there on an errand for Larson. Scarne had only stayed in the town for a short while, but it had been long enough for him to get some impressions of the town. None of which was favourable.

The sun had set and the lamps were already lit in the saloons. As Scarne rode along the main street he could easily see why the town had got its dubious reputation. He must have passed at least a dozen saloons before he reached what he was looking for – the livery stable.

A wizened, grey-haired old-timer gazed at him intently as he approached. As Scarne dismounted he asked, 'What can I do for you, mister?'

'I want to leave my horse here for a few days,' replied Scarne.

'It'll be a dollar a day for oats and water,' said the old man.

'I'll leave it here for a week,' said Scarne producing seven dollars.

'Looks as though you've come a long way,' he said, conversationally, as he accepted the money.

'Could be,' said Scarne, non-committally, as he handed over the reins. As he turned to leave a thought struck him. 'Can you recommend a saloon? One that's not too noisy.'

'Can't say that there are too many of those around,' said the old-timer, as he squinted up at Scarne. 'Your best bet though is probably the Four Horseshoes. It's at the far end of the street.'

Scarne passed several more saloons before he reached it. He also passed a brothel where the ladies of the night were sitting on a bench touting for custom. At his approach one of them jumped up and came up to him.

'Hullo, big boy,' she said, as she blocked his path. 'How would you like to have a good time?'

Even in the fading light and under her layers of make-up he could see that she was past her prime. Not that she probably ever had one, he concluded uncharitably as he went to step round her.

She stepped in front of him, still blocking his way. 'Five dollars for a good time with Dolly,' she stated.

He was tired. He had had a skirmish with Apaches. He had ridden hard all day. The last thing he wanted was a confrontation with an old whore.

'Get out of my way,' he said.

There was something in the tone of his voice which made her obey with alacrity. She stepped aside quickly leaving him room to pass on the side-walk. As he brushed past her and was walking away, she called after him. 'Anyhow you're probably a cissy.' She cackled with laughter at her comment.

The Four Horseshoes was indeed at the end of the street. Its insignia didn't reflect its name since it only had three horseshoes hanging above the door, with a gap where the fourth should have been.

Scarne pushed open the door and stepped inside. To his relief the bar was almost deserted. There were only the inevitable few card-players and a few regulars propping up the bar. Scarne approached the barman.

He was a thin character with a weary moustache and an equally weary expression.

'What will you have?' he asked.

'A beer,' Scarne replied.

He emptied the glass, almost downing the beer in one gulp. He put the glass down like a chess player about to announce checkmate. The barman, who had wandered away to join one of the regulars turned round.

'I'd like a room,' said Scarne.

The weary expression did not change.

31

'I'll find out,' came the reply. He rang a bell. A few moments later a man appeared from inside the saloon.

He was in his fifties with a bald head. He had the same drooping moustache as the barman.

'This guy here wants a room, Dad,' said the barman, jerking an expressive thumb in Scarne's direction.

'How long do you want it for?' asked dad.

'A week,' replied Scarne. 'What about food?'

'My wife will make you an evening meal. In fact she's just cooking it now.'

The room wasn't the best Scarne had stayed in. But it seemed reasonably clean. The owner's wife was a buxom woman. At least she didn't have the same weary expression as her husband and son. In fact she had quite a ready smile. She seemed genuinely pleased that Scarne said he had enjoyed his meal, which he devoured on his own in a small ante-room.

Scarne had a few pints of beer before retiring. He couldn't remember the last time he had had a few beers. It made quite a pleasant change.

CHAPTER 6

When Scarne awoke it took him a few moments to recollect where he was. The previous night he had had a few too many beers. His aching head kept reminding him of that fact.

After washing he strolled out into Main Street. It was bustling with activity. He stood for a few moments in the shelter of the saloon and glanced around. Somewhere among the town's inhabitants were five outlaws. There were probably quite a few more than that in Hawkesville which was rapidly gaining an unenviable reputation as a second Dodge City.

Whereas yesterday it had seemed a perfectly feasible proposition to try to track down the five outlaws and bring them to justice. Today, in the light of the morning air, the idea was definitely flawed. In the first place if he did come across them the odds would be inexorably in their favour. He had never been a bounty hunter before but it would be reasonable to assume that those who followed that profession would concentrate on one outlaw – not five.

He sauntered down the street. He passed several banks, which indicated that Hawkesville was a thriving town. He came to what had once been a theatre, but was now only a burned-out empty shell. This must have been the theatre that Victoria had talked about. He wondered idly whether she had satisfied her ambition in the theatre in Sula.

He arrived at the sheriff's office. It was an imposing stone building which stood apart from the stores on either side. He stared at it for a few moments before coming to a decision. The sign on the door said, 'Knock'. He obeyed and in answer to a barked 'Come in', he stepped inside.

The sheriff was seated behind a large mahogany desk. He was a white-haired man whose several jowls and large stomach testified that he had spent most of his recent life behind his desk.

He stared appraisingly at Scarne. 'What can I do for you, Mister. . . ?'

'Scarne,' he supplied.

'Scarne.' The sheriff tried out the name and filed it away for future reference.

'I'm looking for five men,' said Scarne.

'To work for you?'

'To see them brought to justice.'

'Are you a lawman?' demanded the sheriff, sharply.

'No, a bounty hunter.'

There was a flicker of relief on the sheriff's face as he received the information. Scarne noted it but kept his own face impassive.

'A bounty hunter.' The sheriff savoured the phrase while unwrapping a large cigar. 'You don't look like a bounty hunter,' he added, again giving Scarne the once-over.

'I wouldn't know what one looks like,' said Scarne, drily.

'Well I've met a few,' said the sheriff, conversationally. 'They had one thing in common. They were all killers. You don't look like a killer.'

'I'd kill if I had to,' supplied Scarne.

'If you had to,' said the sheriff, with emphasis. 'There's a difference between having to and killing for money.'

'Five gunmen burned my ranch down,' said Scarne, who was becoming bored with the other's moralizing. 'They killed all my livestock. I aim to find them.'

'Where was this?' demanded the sheriff, putting a match to his cigar.

'A few miles outside Sula.'

'It's outside my jurisdiction.' The sheriff waved a fat hand as he dismissed all territory beyond the radius of the town.

'Can I examine the Wanted notices to see whether the outlaws are on them?' asked Scarne.

'Sure, help yourself.' The sheriff nodded

towards the couple of dozen or so notices which were pinned on the walls.

Scarne began to examine them. The sheriff turned his attention to some telegrams which were on his desk. Scarne scanned the Wanted notices. Most of the outlaws were wanted for murder. Some of them were wanted for robbery – usually a bank. A few were wanted for stealing horses – which carried the same death penalty as the other two crimes.

In the end Scarne turned away. There was no sign of the leader, the short stocky man. He was the one Scarne was sure he would recognize if he came across him again.

'Well?' The sheriff was eyeing Scarne with interest.

'I can't find any of them,' he confessed.

'Do you know any of their names?'

'One of them was called Lewis. Their leader was short and stocky. He had a Texan accent.'

'That's not much to go on.' The sheriff puffed at his cigar.

'I know. I'll just keep on looking.'

'Let me give you some advice, son.' The sheriff leaned forward to emphasize the statement. 'Leave bounty hunting there. It's not a job for an educated man. And I guess you're an educated man. Bounty hunting is for killers. It's for mean men who glory in the sight of blood. Sometimes they might bring in an outlaw. More often than not they end up by getting killed themselves.

'You've said you've lost your ranch; it's a blow, but you could be worse off. You look fit and able. There are plenty of jobs in Hawkesville. I know one or two people who are looking for young men. I could give you a note to introduce yourself to them.'

'Thanks,' said Scarne. 'But I'll stick to my original plan.'

The sheriff stared at him and shook his head sadly. 'You're making a mistake, son,' he said, regretfully. 'If you change your mind, the offer's still open.'

Ten minutes later Scarne was drinking coffee in a coffee shop. He was mulling over the sheriff's suggestion. Maybe the lawman was right. Maybe he should think about getting a job. He was good with his hands. When he had been working in the mine he had had to spend a great deal of his time shoring up the workings. He was used to working with timber. He had seen half a dozen buildings in Hawkesville in various stages of construction. He assumed he could get a job in one of them. Especially if the sheriff recommended him.

Also there was one other flaw in his idea to become a bounty hunter. It seemed likely that none of the outlaws had a bounty on their heads. If so, assuming he captured them, he wouldn't receive any money for delivering them to the law.

He would be putting his life at risk with no possibility of reward at the end.

He finished his coffee and stepped outside the café. Too late he realized that there were five men waiting for him.

'You're coming with us, Scarne,' said their leader.

CHAPTER 7

When Scarne slowly regained consciousness he became aware of several things. In the first place he couldn't move because his arms and legs were tied. Secondly, he was covered with sacks, which prevented him from seeing where he was going. Thirdly, the form of bouncy movement told him that he was lying at the bottom of a cart. A cart which had recently been used to transport pigs, judging by its smell.

They had left him enough space under the sacks for him to breathe – just. He found that if he moved his head to the side one of the sacks covering him ended up against his face. This made breathing difficult. In fact it was so difficult that he hurriedly resumed his previous position. For a few minutes he lay there. The bastards could have killed me if the sacks had fallen on top of me any other way, he thought grimly.

He was gradually aware of the rattle of spurs. It

probably meant that the five were riding their horses, accompanying the cart. Although his head was throbbing as if somebody was regularly hitting it with a hammer, he tried to concentrate on some of the questions which were buzzing around inside it. Firstly, where were they taking him? Secondly, why had they kept him alive? When they had cornered him as he came out of the café he had assumed that his expectation of life had suddenly decreased rapidly, and become a few seconds. They had taken him into the lane which had seemed to confirm his worse fears. Their motive would have been robbery with violence. The particular form of violence ending up in his death. Then he had been hit on the head. And here he was, still alive. For which he was truly thankful.

Shortly afterwards the movement of the cart slowed. It took him several seconds to realize why. Then there was the unmistakable sound of the horses splashing through water. They were crossing a river.

Which river? He listened for the splashing to stop. It went on for a considerable time. It could only mean that it was a wide river. A very wide river. There was only one wide river in this part of the world – the Rio Grande. They were taking him to Mexico.

Suddenly everything fell into place. The outlaws knew his name – Scarne. The girl had informed them of that fact when they had stopped at the

40

farm. The outlaws had come from Mexico. They had heard the story that a man named Scarne had killed his partner, Fernando, a couple of years before when they were working a gold-mine together. There had been an explosion at the mine. Scarne had escaped over the border to Texas. The mine was in a remote part of Mexico. Only Scarne knew exactly where it was.

And here he was going back into Mexico in order to lead them to the mine. It all fitted. At that moment the horses pulled the cart up a steep incline. They were obviously getting out of the river. The upward movement caused the sacks to shift slightly. The one covering Scarne's face slid down far enough for him to see the outside world.

He saw the gang leader riding by the side of the cart. The outlaw suddenly realized that Scarne had recovered consciousness. His face split into a wide grin.

'Welcome to Mexico, Scarne,' he said.

'Why are you keeping me a prisoner?' Scarne demanded, although he was sure he already knew the answer.

'You're going to take us to a gold-mine. Fernando's gold-mine. You're going to make us rich,' came the reply.

One of the other riders began to take an interest in the conversation. 'Is he alive, Manley?' he demanded.

41

'It's all right, Keeson,' came the reply. 'You didn't hit him hard enough to kill him.'

The others laughed.

CHAPTER 8

They pulled up at a clearing a couple of miles further ahead. The five men dismounted.

'You can cut him loose,' Manley indicated Scarne. 'He can't get away from us here.'

When the bonds were removed Scarne rubbed his hands. The others took out their water-bottles and drank deeply. One of the outlaws realized he had emptied his and shook it regretfully.

'You should have filled it when you were riding through the Rio Grande,' Scarne informed him.

'So you know where we are,' said Manley, observing him thoughtfully.

'It doesn't take a genius to work it out,' said Scarne.

'Give him some water,' Manley commanded. Keeson obeyed.

After Scarne had drunk, Manley continued, 'Since you know where we are and you've guessed

43

why we're here, there are some things we'd better sort out.'

'Such as?' said Scarne.

'You're going to lead us to Fernando's mine. We don't want any trouble with you. If we have any we'll shoot you. Do I make myself clear?'

'Perfectly,' supplied Scarne.

'If, however, we get the gold from the mine it will be split six ways. That's a promise.'

Scarne knew that as far as promises went it was about as reliable as Saint Peter's when he said he wouldn't deny Jesus.

'Have we got a deal?' demanded Manley.

'Sure,' lied Scarne.

'Right. Now you're the mining expert. We're the beginners. The next thing we've got to do is to go into San Caldiz to get the equipment we'll need to work the mine. We'll need a list from you of the things we'll want.'

'Give me a pencil and paper,' said Scarne.

Manley gave a nod of satisfaction at seeing how readily Scarne had accepted the situation. In fact the reason for Scarne's acceptance was that he had his own motive for going back to the mine. He was convinced that there was still gold there. If he could manage to get at it, he would devise some plan to get rid of the outlaws. Permanently. After all that was what they were planning to do to him if he managed to extract the gold.

Scarne started making the list. He had put down

44

a few items when he paused. He shook his head.

'This won't work,' he stated. 'I'll have to come into San Caldiz with you. I'll have to pick timbers to shore up the roof. You won't know what I want. We could end up with timbers that would collapse half an hour after we'd put them up.'

Manley scowled. It was obvious that he didn't like anything or anyone interfering with his decisions.

'It sounds reasonable,' said Lewis. 'We'll all be there to keep an eye on him.'

'It won't be necessary,' said Scarne. 'I want to get at that gold as much as all of you do. It's the one thing I've dreamed about since I went back over the border.'

Manley stared at Scarne intently while he tried to make up his mind. At last he said, 'What have we got to lose? You're the one whose got everything to lose. If we turn you over to the Mexican police they'll throw you in jail. You'll probably rot there knowing how long they take to bring you to trial. When they finally try you, you'll be found guilty and hanged. No, you wouldn't dare step out of line,' said Manley with a grin.

The others smiled too, relieved that Manley had accepted the situation, and ended up in a good humour. Their boss's fits of temper were events which it were better to avoid at all costs.

Half an hour later they rode into San Caldiz. Scarne was riding the spare horse. It was a chestnut mare which bore no comparison to the black stallion which he had been forced to leave behind in the corral in Hawkesville. Still, beggars can't be choosers, he observed, philosophically.

San Caldiz was a bustling town. Scarne had spent several days there two years ago before he had started on his way to Fernando's mine. He knew there were some pretty *señoritas*, here. One of them, Rosita, had especially caught his eye. In fact they had met on a couple of occasions and Scarne had hoped that the occasions would increase together with Rosita's ardour. Their relationship had become close and showed every promise of becoming closer. Then Scarne had discovered that Rosita's father was the chief of the police and the discovery had suddenly succeeded in putting some considerable distance between them. Shortly afterwards he had started out for Fernando's mine.

These thoughts flitted through his head as the six men rode down the wide main street. Not for the first time he wondered why the main street was wider than the main street in, say, Hawkesville or Sula. Maybe it was just that the Mexicans liked plenty of space. Their town square, too, was bigger, he reflected, as they rode into it.

There was a hardware shop on the far corner of the square. Scarne had bought his supplies there two years before. There was a faint chance that the owner might recognize him. But it was a chance he had to take in order to buy the materials he needed.

He need not have worried about the owner recognizing him – he was served by another member of the family. He ordered the timber he needed. The digging implements and the dynamite completed the order. Scarne supervised their loading on to the cart.

When the operation was completed, Scarne waited with the other outlaws while Manley stayed behind to pay the shopkeeper. When Manley finally came out his face was grim. He quickly swung up on his horse.

'Let's get out of here,' he snapped.

'Did you pay him?' enquired Scarne.

'Where do you think I had the money to pay him?' hissed Manley.

'If you've killed him we'll have the police after us,' growled Scarne.

'I don't need you to tell me that,' snarled Manley.

CHAPTER 9

'How many days travelling will it take us before we reach your mine?' demanded the Frenchman, Leguin.

Scarne shrugged. 'Nine days . . . ten days.'

'Do we come to any other towns before we get there?' asked Keeson.

'There's a small town called Verde. It's in the mountains. Not many people visit it.'

'Sounds like the town where I was brought up,' said Garby. He was obviously the comedian of the party.

After that brief outburst conversation lulled. The first part of the journey lay across the semi-desert. It was a wild and inhospitable region. There was no sign of human habitation. There was also no sign of any following police posse. They were heading towards the mountains which could just be seen in the distance.

They were now travelling at a steady pace, not

pushing the horses. After travelling for some time they rode past the bones of some dead animal which had been picked clean by the vultures.

'What do you reckon it was?' asked Keeson.

'Coyote,' said Scarne, succinctly.

'I thought they always travelled in packs,' said Leguin.

'They do,' replied Scarne. 'But if one of them can't keep up for some reason or other they set on it. They kill it and eat it.'

'Nice friendly animals,' said Lewis.

'Make sure we don't set on you if you step out of line.' Manley addressed Scarne.

'I wouldn't fancy eating him. He looks too tough,' said Garby, amid laughter.

It took them three days before they reached the foothills of the mountains.

'I hope there's some water here,' said Leguin, 'My water bottle's empty.'

'My stomach's empty,' said Garby. This time nobody laughed.

They camped in the shade of a clump of cotton-woods. There was sufficient grass for the horses to feed on. There was a stream running nearby from which they had all filled their water-bottles.

Keeson voiced their collective thoughts. 'Whew! I'm glad to get away from the desert,' he stated.

'There should be some game up in these mountains, shouldn't there?' asked Garby. 'I'm fed up with eating these dry biscuits.'

'There could be some game,' stated Scarne. 'Maybe a deer, wild boar or even a buffalo.'

'I tasted buffalo-meat once in Tuscon,' said Lewis. 'It was like a steak. It was quite tasty.'

'A steak. Just think of it,' said Garby, reflectively.

'Even if we shot a buffalo you'd have to hang it for three days before we could start cutting it up,' said Scarne.

'We can forget about it,' said Manley. 'We'll be on our way first thing in the morning.'

'So it's back to dried biscuit,' said Garby, regretfully.

In fact they managed to shoot a few rabbits on their travels up into the mountains during the next few days. They would cook them on their fire in the evenings.

'I'm getting quite good at skinning a rabbit,' Garby announced.

A few days later they could see a village in the distance.

'Verde,' Scarne informed them.

As they neared the town they could see that it comprised the usual collection of adobe houses.

'Where's the nearest cantina?' demanded Lewis.

Manley reined in his horse and the others followed suit. 'We'll have a few drinks in a cantina,' he said. 'I think we all deserve it after our journey to get here.'

'And a plate of hot tortillas,' said Garby. 'My mouth's watering already.'

'But no mixing with the local women. That means you, Leguin.'

'Who, me?' demanded the Frenchman, innocently. The others grinned.

'We'll be starting first thing in the morning,' continued Manley. 'How many more days' travelling is it?' He addressed the question to Scarne.

'A couple of hours.'

'Good.'

They rode into Verde to dozens of curious stares. It seemed that most of the inhabitants had come out to see the six riders. Nearly all the onlookers were Mexicans, although there was a smattering of Indian faces to be seen here and there. Everyone kept close to their front doors as though ready to make a bolt inside if the riders proved to be *bandidos*. On the other hand maybe they were hunters. Maybe the two covered waggons held the guns with which they intended hunting for buffalo – or even wild boars. If they were hunters maybe they would bring some much needed fresh meat into the town. The men in the town were hopeless hunters. They went up into the mountains to hunt, but the most they ever came back with was the odd deer. Their excuse was that the Apaches were camped up in the mountain. The last thing the men wanted to do was to start a battle with the Apaches. If they did many of the women of the town would surely become widows. Then the Apaches would take advantage of the fact that there would be only a handful of able-bodied men left. They would attack the town. They would undoubtedly be the victors if such an attack were made. Which would mean that the Apaches would take over the town. And everything in it. Including the women. And everyone knew what the fate of the women would be in the hands of the Apaches.

The watchers saw the six riders dismount near Maria's cantina. They tied their horses to the hitching rail. One of the men sat on the stone seat. He was evidently going to keep guard.

The others approached the door, which was suddenly opened. The onlookers guessed that Maria had been watching their approach though her window. She stared at the five men who were standing there. Suddenly her expression changed. Her face split into a wide grin.

'Scarne! I knew you'd come back. And this is your son,' she cried, triumphantly.

CHAPTER 10

Scarne stared in disbelief at the young child who had appeared behind his mother. She picked him up and showed him proudly to Scarne. He was about eighteen months old; a well-built half-caste with brown curly hair. His coal-black eyes stared suspiciously at Scarne.

'His name is Juan,' announced his mother.

The five outlaws had been gazing at the scene as it unfolded. They now began to smile as its full implication dawned on them. Then they began to laugh. They were soon howling with laughter. They were laughing so much that a couple of them had to hold their sides.

'You left a memento behind the last time you came here,' gasped Lewis in between bouts of laughter.

Maria's eyes flashed with rage. 'If your friends think it is funny then they are not welcome in my cantina,' she stormed.

She was about to shut the door when Scarne managed to keep it open with his foot.

'Let's talk this over, Maria,' he begged.

She thawed a little. 'All right,' she conceded. 'Your friends can come inside the bar. But I want to see you in the kitchen,' she added, pointedly.

The outlaws went into the bar where they were served by a Mexican whom Scarne vaguely remembered as one of Maria's brothers. Scarne took a seat in the kitchen and waited for Maria to break the silence. She hesitated for a few moments as though searching for the right words. At last she started:

'When we became lovers I assumed that you would be staying in Verde. You were in charge of the mine and I thought that when you reached the gold you would stay here. We would even get married.' She stared at him solemnly. Juan, too, was regarding him intently.

'I had every intention of staying here,' averred Scarne. 'But you know it didn't work out.'

'I never believed that you killed Fernando to have his share of the gold,' she continued. 'I don't believe you're that sort of person.'

'You're right. I didn't kill him. One of the miners named Lomez killed him. They had been playing cards while they were waiting for me to set the explosives. Fernando had had an amazing run of cards. He had won every hand. Lomez owed him over a thousand dollars – American dollars. In

56

the end Lomez accused Fernando of cheating. He had a quick temper. He went for his gun. Fernando didn't have a gun. He ran back into the mine. Lomez shot him.'

'But why did you run away? You could have explained to the authorities that you weren't the one responsible for killing Fernando.'

Juan had now come out from the protective skirt of his mother. He was standing by Scarne's side. On impulse Scarne picked him up and put him on his knee. For a second it looked as though the boy might jump down. But he changed his mind and gazed up at Scarne, wonderingly. Maria's face lit up on seeing the family scene.

'I was the only American working in the mine. The men resented me because we hadn't struck gold. They were a lazy lot and I had to keep on bullying them to get them to work. They hadn't been paid for three weeks. There were rumours that it was an unlucky mine. Nobody had seen the shooting. I had been the nearest to the two card players. When I walked out of the mine I could tell from the men's expressions that they thought I had killed Fernando. Of course Lomez had disappeared through another passageway. I don't suppose he's ever been heard of since.'

Maria's face wore a thoughtful expression. 'Why did you blow the mine up?' she demanded.

'I didn't. It was an accident. I had set a couple of fuses. These were burning away as I went in to get

Fernando's body. It was dark in the mine and I couldn't find his body. I knew I only had a few seconds to get back out of the mine. When I did the men were pointing their revolvers at me.'

'They thought that you killed Fernando,' supplied Maria.

'That's right. He was very popular around here.'

'When he first discovered the mine he used to give us little gold nuggets,' said Maria, dreamily. 'He used to tell us to keep them because they would soon be worth a lot of money.'

'That was fool's gold,' stated Scarne.

'You mean they were not worth anything?' demanded Maria, indignantly.

'No more than any pebble you can find outside the cantina. As I said the men were pointing their guns at me. I pleaded with them to go back and work the mine. They had all had enough. They were happy to let the mine blow up. They said there wasn't any gold there anyhow.'

'It was a big bang,' said Maria, with a smile. 'Bang,' she waved her arms to show Juan how big it had been. He smiled too.

'The mood of the miners was ugly,' continued Scarne. 'They blamed me for not having found the gold. My guns were in my saddle-bag.'

'But you managed to escape?'

'I had a couple of pieces of dynamite left in the pouch on my belt. I took one out and lit it. They stared at it for a moment then they turned tail and

58

began to run. They knew enough about dynamite to know that if it blew up we would all be killed.'

'So what did you do then?' Her voice had become colder.

'I jumped on my horse and rode away.'

'You could have stopped here and explained what had happened.' The coldness had now become distinctly icy.

'The miners were after my blood. I had to get away as quickly as I could.'

'I would have been prepared to come with you,' she stated, flatly.

'I was in a hurry.'

'Yes, you've always been in a hurry, haven't you, Scarne,' she said, bitterly. 'Perhaps that's your problem.' She took the boy from him and the pair disappeared into a back room.

CHAPTER 11

The outlaws were all for staying at the cantina and enjoying the wine and tortillas. However when they had had enough to eat Manley ordered them brusquely to move.

'We're going to the mine,' he said.

There were mutterings of discontent, but in the end the men obeyed their leader and mounted their horses. Scarne too jumped up on the chestnut mare.

'Will you be back?' demanded Maria.

'Sure,' replied Scarne.

'You said that the last time,' she said, accusingly.

'Go on, give her a kiss,' said Leguin.

Scarne hesitated then jumped down from his horse. He took Maria in his arms and she responded with a passionate embrace.

'There'll be plenty of time for that when we've got the gold,' snapped Manley.

'*Vive l'amour*,' said Leguin, as they rode away from the cantina.

The camp was as Scarne had left it two years before. There were the same dilapidated miners' huts, except that they were now overgrown with weeds. There was the same shaft, which had been filled in with rocks after the explosion. Scarne was relieved to see that the mountain stream which flowed through the mine was low enough not to prove a hindrance to their digging. At one time when he had been working the mine the stream had become a raging torrent after some heavy rain and they had been forced to abandon their digging for several days. That was when he had found solace with Maria. He sighed at the thought.

'You say there's gold in there?' demanded Manley. The two men were standing just outside the entrance to the mine. The others had selected a hut and were busy pulling up the weeds, preparatory to making the hut hospitable.

'There's gold in there,' affirmed Scarne. 'I'd stake my life on it.'

Manley scratched his chin thoughtfully. 'It's going to take us ages to shift this rubble before we can even start digging,' he observed.

'If we had had another dozen men it would help,' suggested Scarne.

'Then we'll have to get them,' stated Manley.

'You'd have to pay them,' Scarne pointed out.

'That's no problem. It just happened that the guy who owned the hardware store also had a safe under the counter. I persuaded him to let me have the combination before I killed him,' he concluded, casually.

'You bastard,' snarled Scarne.

Manley's face twisted into a scowl. He stepped close to Scarne.

'Let's get this straight,' he snapped. 'I'm in charge here. I'll do things my way. If anyone steps out of line, I've got my own way of dealing with them. And that includes you.' He turned on his heel and headed for one of the shacks.

Scarne took a deep breath. Don't step out of line. That was good advice. He'd have to tread a narrow path until they had found the gold. The name of the game was to hold his tongue. He'd have to bide his time. He'd need the five outlaws to help to get at the gold. If Manley could get another dozen men from the town that would help matters considerably.

Leguin now joined him by the entrance to the cave.

'Is there enough gold in there to make us all rich?' he demanded.

'Enough to make you rich twice over,' stated Scarne.

'All I want is enough money to pay for a passage back to *la belle France*,' said Leguin.

'What will you do when you get back there?'

63

asked Scarne, as he rolled a cigarette.

'I'm going to open a restaurant in Paris,' said the Frenchman, dreamily. 'I'm going to marry a French girl. She must be able to cook. She must be pretty, with dark curly hair. I don't mind if she's plump. Most of these American girls are too skinny for my taste.'

Scarne smiled at the Frenchman's picture of his ideal woman.

'Leguin, if we get out all the gold that's in that mine, you'll have enough money to open half a dozen restaurants,' he stated.

CHAPTER 12

The following morning Manley and Keeson went into Verde to recruit some helpers while Scarne supervised clearing some of the rocks at the entrance to the mine. He had stripped to the waist and the others followed suit. Scarne attacked the rocks with gusto. He was glad to be doing some physical work at last. True, he had kept himself occupied while on Larsen's farm with chopping down trees and building the barns, but that had been light work compared with this. He relished the challenge of moving some of the big rocks. If the others baulked at trying to move any of the rocks because of their size, he would take over and move the rock himself. The fact that he was prepared to do his share of the work, or rather more than his fair share, meant that the outlaws soon accepted him as their leader.

It was obvious that none of the three was used to hard physical labour. After they had been working for a couple of hours Scarne called a rest.

'Not before time,' said Lewis. 'I've got muscles aching where I didn't know I had muscles before.'

'Mining is hard work,' said Scarne. 'But it will all be worth it when you see the shining yellow stuff.'

Scarne let them have a longer break than he would normally have allowed his workers. In fact they were still relaxing on the grass when Manley and Keeson arrived back. It was obvious that Manley was in a bad mood.

'I thought you were supposed to be putting them to work,' he snapped.

'They've been working,' replied Scarne. 'They're having a rest, since they're not used to hard work.'

'You are, I suppose,' snarled Manley.

'He's worked twice as hard as we have,' supplied Lewis. 'We've cleared all those rocks.' He pointed to the pile of rocks which they had moved.

'Where are the helpers?' asked Scarne.

It was Keeson who answered. 'We couldn't get any.'

'Why not?' demanded Scarne, with interest.

'They say the mine's unlucky,' retorted Manley. 'They're not prepared to work here.'

'How much did you offer them?' asked Scarne.

'A dollar a day. That's what they would get if they were working on a ranch in America.'

Scarne smiled.

'You think it's funny, do you?' snapped Manley. 'Well it won't be so funny since we've got to move all these rocks ourselves.'

'Who was the guy you were dealing with?' demanded Scarne.

'His name was Soldero. He's a big guy.'

'Yes, I know him,' replied Scarne, thoughtfully. 'He's playing a game with you.

'Well, whatever he's playing, I don't think it's funny.'

'He knows you'll be back, With a larger offer.'

'I'm not going back,' growled Manley.

'We can't shift all these rocks ourselves,' wailed Lewis.

'I could go and see if I can persuade him,' suggested Scarne.

Manley appeared to waver.

'Let him try,' suggested Keeson. 'We've got nothing to lose.'

'All right,' said Manley, coming to a decision. 'You go back with him. You'd better offer them two dollars a day,' he added, reluctantly.

Scarne and Keeson rode back into Verde. There was no conversation between the two, Scarne still holding Keeson responsible for the crack on the head which he had received.

In the town square a group of men were gathered.

'Those are the ones that Manley tried to persuade to come back with us,' supplied Keeson.

'And the big guy in the front is Soldero.'

'Right,' said Scarne. 'Let me handle this.'

He reined in his horse in front of the big Mexican, who stood with arms folded and a sneer on his face.

'Are you in charge of these men?' demanded Scarne.

'You know I am,' replied the other.

'Then tell your men to come to work at the mine. They will get a dollar a day.'

'That's not enough,' snapped Soldero.

'I say it is.' Scarne delivered the statement slowly and deliberately.

The twenty or so men looked on interestedly.

'It's not enough,' reiterated Soldero.

'I say you're a liar. The men are prepared to accept the payment.'

The men who had been listening to the discussion now tensed with the sudden realization that something was about to happen.

'If you'd get down from that horse I'll show you who's a liar,' snarled Soldero.

'Give him the extra money,' whispered Keeson.

Scarne ignored him and jumped down from the horse. A circle of spectators appeared around the two men as if by magic.

Scarne slowly took off his jacket. He tossed it casually to the floor. Soldero was already in his shirt. His face split into a wide grin. He was the champion fighter in Verde. He had won dozens of fights and was also the undisputed champion in arm-wrestling.

'I'll make you eat your words, gringo,' he announced, as he began slowly to circle round Scarne.

Scarne had adopted the stance of the fighters he had seen in travelling circuses over the border. He was sideways on to Soldero. This gave him the advantage of his longer reach, although Soldero was a couple of stone heavier than Scarne.

The advantage of Scarne's stance was apparent when he began to jab Soldero in the face as the other circled him trying to find an opening so that he could rush inside. At first Soldero pretended that Scarne's jabs didn't bother him. He even managed to grin at the first few jabs. But when they became more persistent his grin changed to a scowl. The scowl then changed to outright fury. With a roar he threw caution to the wind and headed towards Scarne.

Scarne sidestepped his charge effortlessly. He hit him hard in the stomach. The blow, although delivered with all Scarne's thirteen stone behind it, apparently just bounced off Soldero. This time Soldero did grin happily.

Scarne was nonplussed. He hesitated for a moment while deciding what form of attack he should proceed with. The slight hesitation almost proved to be his downfall. Soldero seized his opportunity. He caught Scarne with haymaker of a blow in the stomach. The impact spun Scarne round. For a few moments he struggled to keep on his feet. The crowd, which had been silent up to then, suddenly became vociferous. There was no doubt whose side they were on. It was Soldero's.

He moved in for the kill. Scarne was still gasping for breath. Soldero licked his lips in the pleasurable anticipation of finishing off the gringo. Scarne's legs had now stopped wobbling. But he knew instinctively that he was in no condition to carry on with the fight at that moment. As Soldero closed in, Scarne adopted a ploy he had seen the circus fighters use. He suddenly moved in close and hung on to Soldero.

The Mexican was surprised by the sudden change of tactics. He tried to shrug Scarne off, but he hung on grimly. 'Stand up and fight, gringo,' hissed Soldero.

Scarne hung on. He realized that the strength was returning to his legs. Soldero began to taunt him. 'If I'd wanted a dancing partner, I'd have chosen a *señorita*,' he growled.

There was appreciative laughter from the audience, which had now swollen in size. Scarne was tempted to let go of Soldero, but he realized that every second he could hang on to him meant that his strength would be returning. Finally, Soldero, playing to the audience, turned his head towards Scarne and gave him a kiss on the cheek. The audience roared with laughter. Scarne chose that moment to step away. Soldero began to smile at the success of his ploy. His smile didn't last long. Scarne hit him on the jaw.

It was a perfect upper cut; the kind of blow that would have floored most men. But not Soldero, although this time it was his turn for his legs to wobble. Scarne seized his opportunity gratefully. He began to rain blows into Soldero's face. The Mexican was largely defenceless as he tried ineffectively to parry the blows. Scarne stepped in time and time again, aiming for Soldero's face. Nearly all his blows landed.

Soldero's face was soon a mass of blood. He had cuts under both eyes. The crowd had grown silent at the sight of their champion being unmercifully beaten. Soldero did try to stop Scarne's blows with a few more haymakers, but one of his eyes was now closed and he couldn't clearly see the figure who was inflicting such pain and humiliation on him.

Scarne realized that he, too, was tiring. The strain of delivering so many blows together with the body-blow he had received from Soldero had taken its toll. He eyed the staggering figure in front of him, sizing him up for one final upper cut. The opportunity finally presented itself. He delivered the blow perfectly. For a second it appeared as though Soldero was not going to go down. Then his legs slowly began to buckle. After hitting the floor he rolled over so that he was lying on his back.

Scarne put his foot on Soldero's chest. He knew that he had nothing to fear from the Mexican.

'Are all you men ready to work for a dollar a day?' He addressed the assembled workers.

There was a general chorus of agreement.

'Right, then you'll start straightaway. You'll go with Mr Keeson here to the mine.'

The men trooped away to fetch their horses. Scarne observed that the alacrity with which they did so pointed to the fact that they were in fact eager to work. He turned to Keeson.

'I've got some business to see to here. I'll be along later.'

He read in Keeson's expression that the man was about to argue. Then Keeson changed his mind. He accepted Scarne's decision with a shrug.

'What about him?' he pointed to the bloodied Soldero, who was just staggering to his feet.

'He won't bother us again,' said Scarne.

CHAPTER 13

Having collected his jacket Scarne headed for the cantina. The crowd of onlookers were slowly dispersing. Some of then glanced briefly at Scarne, although no one spoke to him.

He arrived at the cantina and knocked at the door. After a few moments Maria opened it. She regarded him steadily.

'Yes?'

'Aren't you going to invite me in?'

'Why should I, after that exhibition in the square?'

'You saw it?' Scarne passed a weary hand over his brow.

She stared at him. 'I'm glad you beat Soldero. He is a bully. He thinks he's God's gift to women.'

'Then what are you complaining about?' He could still detect the displeasure in her voice.

'Your final gesture of putting your foot on him.

It so humiliated him that he would have lost much face. You know what that means?'

'No, but you're going to tell me.'

'He won't rest until he gets his revenge. You'll have to watch yourself day and night.'

'I promise I'll do that. Now, can I come in and have a wash. And maybe something to eat and drink.'

'Come into the kitchen.'

A kettle was warming on the fire. Maria poured some of the water into a large bowl. Scarne stripped to the waist and began to wash himself.

'You're going to have a nice bruise there,' she observed, indicating the area where Soldero's body-blow had landed.

'I've had worse,' said Scarne, reaching for a towel.

'Here, let me.' Maria took the towel from him and began to dry his back.

They were standing close together. Maria leaned forward and lightly kissed his shoulder. Scarne didn't respond. Her answer was to dig her teeth into him.

'You vixen.' Scarne spun round and seized her. Suddenly they were in a passionate embrace.

When they broke apart Maria said dreamily, 'It's been a long time.'

'We can make up for it,' said Scarne, kissing her neck.

Just at that moment Juan chose to come into the

kitchen. Maria moved quickly out of Scarne's embrace.

Scarne gave an exasperated sigh at the interruption.

'You're partly responsible for him,' said Maria, pointedly, as she picked the boy up.

'Yeah, well I'd better get back to the mine,' said Scarne, still harbouring frustration.

'Stay and have a meal,' pleaded Maria.

Scarne was undecided. Juan held out his hand as though echoing his mother's invitation. After hesitating for a moment, Scarne took hold of the boy's hand. Maria's face split into a smile.

While Maria was preparing the tortillas Scarne began to toss a ball to Juan. After missing the first couple of times, Juan managed to catch the next one. Scarne smiled at him encouragingly. The game continued for several minutes with Scarne giving the boy encouraging smiles every time he caught the ball. Now and then Maria glanced up from her cooking and smiled at them proudly.

While Scarne was eating his meal with evident relish, Maria coughed. It was the sort of cough which was obviously a prelude to an announcement. Scarne glanced up at her curiously.

'I've got a suggestion,' she said.

'Go ahead,' said Scarne, tucking into another tortilla.

'I suggest we should get away from here.'

Scarne was obviously going to protest, but she silenced him with a wave of her hand. 'Hear me out. If you succeeded in getting the gold out, do you think the outlaws will let you live to have your share of it? No. You will be killed as soon as they've got the gold. There are five of them and only one of you, so the chances are they will succeed in killing you.'

'Thank you for your faith in my future,' said Scarne, drily.

'So I suggest we get out now. Before you get killed. I'd rather have you alive so that you can carry on playing with Juan. He needs a father.' The first few statements had been delivered in a flat voice, but now she became emotional. 'We could go to Topez. It's a long journey but I'm sure we could make it. I've got some cousins there. I've also saved some money. We'd be safe. We could open a cantina. Please, Scarne.'

She was now kneeling by his chair and holding his hand.

He detached his hand gently. 'There's only one snag with your plan.'

'What's that?'

'Manley and his men would follow us. Without me they can't work the mine. They'd soon catch up with us. They'd make sure that I didn't try to escape again by killing you and Juan.'

Maria's eyes widened. She stood up. 'They'd do that?'

'They would. The only way I can keep us all alive is by going along with their plan.'

CHAPTER 14

Scarne rode slowly back to the mine. The Mexicans were busily clearing away the fallen rocks. When Scarne dismounted Manley came over to him.

'How long do you think it will take to clear this rubbish away?'

'Two or three days, maybe. It depends how much damage has been done to the roof inside the mine.'

Manley regarded him keenly. 'How is that you know so much about mining?'

'I was brought up on stories about gold-mining. My grandfather was one of the forty-niners. I could recognize gold from fool's gold when I was six years old.'

'What's our next step?' demanded Manley.

'Get your men to fix up their shacks while the Mexicans are clearing the mine. Most of them have got holes in the roof. If it starts raining here it could last for days.'

Manley called to his men. 'Scarne here says that you had better fix the roofs of your shacks. It could start to rain. If it does you'll all get wet.'

'If it rains we could go into Verde,' suggested Leguin.

'We'll all stay here until we get the gold out,' snapped Manley.

Scarne went over to supervise the shifting of the rocks. He recognized a few of the men as having worked for him before. One of them, Perez, stopped working and looked up at him.

'The Apaches are watching us,' he stated.

Scarne glanced at the top of the mountain above them. There was no sign of any Indians.

'When did you see them?' he demanded.

'When we came out here. They were up on the top of the rise there.' He pointed to a peak high above them.

'They were always watching us when we were working the mine before,' said Scarne, thoughtfully.

'Yes, but things are different now,' stated Perez.

'In what way?' demanded Scarne.

'The Apaches had used the caves in the mine as burial places.'

'Yes, I know. We found some of their bones in the caves.'

'But we didn't disturb them.'

'Of course not. They didn't bother us. Although a few of the workers claimed that they saw an Apache ghost in the caves.'

'But when the mine was blown up it did disturb the bones,' said Perez, slowly.

'I see,' said Scarne, thoughtfully. 'You think it could make a difference.'

'The Apaches have always worshipped their ancestors. They probably weren't too happy about us working in the mine, but they waited to see what was going to happen. Now of course the situation has changed. The explosion disturbed their ancestors' bones. They'll never forgive you.'

'You mean us,' said Scarne, drily.

'No, they know that you were the person in charge. Even though the mine belonged to Fernando. You're the one they'll be gunning for.'

'I'll keep it in mind,' said Scarne.

He went over to the shack where he had spent the previous night. It was next to Manley's, who was nailing up his broken roof.

'I've got some news,' said Scarne.

'What is it?' demanded Manley, as he stopped working for a moment.

'The Apaches are watching us.'

Manley automatically glanced up at the ridge above. 'They're no threat, are they?'

'I'm afraid they are. When the mine was blown up it disturbed the bones of their ancestors who had been buried in the complex of caves.'

81

'I see,' said Manley, thoughtfully. 'We had trouble with the Apaches in Texas. Once they get an idea in their heads they don't give up. They keep on coming back.'

'So tell the men to keep a loaded gun by their sides at night,' stated Scarne.

'You don't know how many there are, do you?' demanded Manley.

'Not yet. One of the men, Perez, spotted them. They probably only had a few in sight. The rest would have been hiding down behind the ridge. We won't know how many there are until they attack us.'

'You're a real Job's comforter,' stated Manley, turning back to his work on the roof.

CHAPTER 15

Trouble, when it came, arrived a couple of days later. Not in the form of any Apaches but in the shapely figure of Maria. She rode up to the mine. Scarne was busy helping to shift a particularly stubborn rock. He looked up at her approach.

She jumped down from her horse. The men stopped work as they watched her approach Scarne. She stopped in front of him. They stood motionless regarding each other for a few moments.

'Well, aren't you going to kiss me?' demanded Maria.

Scarne kissed her. What he had intended as a perfunctory kiss somehow turned into a lingering one. There were appreciative whistles from the Mexicans. Leguin too joined them in an appreciative whistle. Manley scowled and came over to them.

'What are you doing here?' he snarled. 'Only

men are allowed on the site.'

'I've come to bring you some news,' said Maria, coolly. 'Of course if you don't want to hear it, I'll go back.'

'No, hang on,' said Scarne. 'What's the news?'

'A man came to the cantina this morning. He didn't say who he was, but I'm sure he's a policeman.'

'How do you know he's a policeman?' demanded Manley.

'I've worked in a cantina for years, I can smell them. The same way I can smell an outlaw.'

Manley scowled. 'Be careful, young lady. Your tongue will get you into trouble. And you won't always have this guy around to protect you.' He turned on his heel and stalked away.

Scarne let Maria into his shack.

'It's not very comfortable, is it,' she said, critically, as she surveyed the bare single room.

'It'll do for the next few weeks.' He sat on the floor and Maria came over to sit by him. 'Now tell me about this policeman.'

'He's not from around here. I'm positive about that. Our local policemen don't know him either. One of them was in the cantina and he told me he didn't recognize him.'

'Perhaps he wasn't a policeman after all,' suggested Scarne.

Maria flared up. 'I'm telling you he's a policeman.'

84

'All right,' conceded Scarne. 'In that case you've got yourself a job.'

'What is it?'

'Find out as much as you can about him. Use your feminine charms.'

'You think I've got charms,' she said, coyly.

'There's no doubt about it. Look how you charmed me in the first place.'

She bristled. 'You – you—' She aimed a blow at him. He caught her hand and they sat as still as statues for a few moments. Then he pulled her towards him. The next moment they were kissing passionately.

'Someone might come in,' she said, after they had come up for air.

'They'd have to knock first. There's no way I'd let them in while I've got some unfinished business.'

'What's the unfinished business?' she demanded, huskily. Their faces were close together. Her hair brushed his chin.

'It's something we started a couple of years ago,' he said, suggestively.

'How do I know you won't go off and leave me again?' she asked.

He was kissing her neck. 'I swear I won't leave you this time.'

'Then you'll marry me?'

'I always intended to.'

She hastily slipped off her dress. The figure

underneath was firm and perfectly proportioned.

'I'd forgotten how beautiful you are,' he said, admiringly.

She searched his face as though seeking confirmation that he really did mean what he said. Finally she stretched out on the floor.

'What are you waiting for?' she asked.

CHAPTER 16

The following day the rains came. It was heavy, persistent, driving rain. The sort of rain that would soak a workman to the skin in a couple of minutes. The Mexicans laid down their tools and hastily sought to shelter inside the mine.

Scarne joined them. 'It looks as though this is going to keep up for a few hours,' he observed.

'A few days, *señor*,' said one of the workmen. There was a chorus of agreement from the others.

Scarne stared at the sky. It was as inhospitable as the surrounding mountains.

'What are we going to do?' asked Perez, who had adopted the position of spokesman for the workers.

'There's not much point in staying here watching it rain. You'd better all go back to town. I want you all here first thing in the morning.'

The Mexicans headed for their horses. At that moment Manley appeared on the scene.

'Who said they could go off?' he shouted.

'I did,' said Scarne. 'They can't do anything here today. If this rain keeps up we'll be lucky if they do anything here tomorrow either.'

Manley's face was twisted with anger. 'I'm the one in charge here. I'm the one to tell the workers to go.'

'All right, you can tell them next time,' conceded Scarne, turning on his heel.

'Don't walk away when I'm talking to you,' yelled Manley.

'There's something more important in the mine than talking to you,' retorted Scarne. He entered the shaft again. He had to step aside to avoid the stream. Whereas before the storm it had been a low trickle, it was now a substantial flow of water a few inches deep. He stared at it thoughtfully.

'What are you looking for?' demanded Manley, irritably.

'This stream could spoil our whole plan,' stated Scarne.

'How?' demanded a puzzled Manley.

'It all depends on how much it rises. If it rises too much then it could flood the mine. We'd never be able to work it then.'

'Has it flooded before?'

'I don't know. I'd have to ask Maria.'

'You keep away from Maria. At least until we've got all the gold out of the mine,' said Manley, threateningly.

In fact Maria's thoughts were very much centred on Scarne as she went about her daily tasks in the cantina. Her mind dwelt on their love-making yesterday. It had been wonderful. She hugged herself at the recollection of just how perfect it had been. Scarne was quite a man, there was no doubt about that. The only thing that niggled in her mind was whether he would keep his promise and marry her.

She knew that in the eyes of the church she had committed a sin by letting Scarne make love to her. She knew also that she would have to go to church one day and confess her sin. But not for a few days. During that time she would be remembering their love with pleasure. Then, of course, she would have to confess it to the padre and that would make it a sin. She often wondered why things were like that. Many things that she liked doing were called sins by the church. Ah, well, it was all beyond her comprehension. All she knew was that yesterday their love-making had been perfect and the church could say what they liked about it.

There was one other thing on her mind. Scarne had told her to try to find out about the man who, she insisted, was a policeman. He had told her to use her feminine charms on him. She smiled at the recollection.

As if in answer to her contemplation the man himself came into the cantina half an hour later. He was dripping wet.

'I never knew it rained like this up in the mountains,' he said, taking off his hat and shaking it.

'Give me your coat,' said Maria, with a welcoming smile. 'I'll dry it in the kitchen.'

'That's kind of you,' said the stranger, taking off his coat and handing it to her.

'I won't be a moment,' said Maria. 'I'll get you a drink when I come back.'

She hurried into the kitchen. She tossed the stranger's hat on to a chair near the fire. She delved into one of the pockets of the coat. It was empty. She tried the other one. There was nothing there either. Regretfully she draped the coat over the chair so that its back was facing the fire.

Back in the bar she asked the stranger, with a smile, what he would like to drink. He ordered tequila.

'Leave the bottle here,' he ordered.

There was no one else in the bar, so she was able to observe him undisturbed. She did not directly stare at him, but watched him through the mirror above her. The stranger was quite tall, almost as tall as Scarne. That was the first thing which had aroused her suspicions about him. Most Mexicans were rather short and stocky.

She studied him carefully. He had a thin face with a thin moustache. She decided that it was not an attractive face. Certainly not handsome, like her Scarne.

After he had drunk a couple of glasses of tequila he spoke to Maria.

'Won't you join me in a drink?'

She hesitated. Normally she would have refused the offer straight away. But she remembered Scarne's advice to try to find out as much as she could about the stranger.

'I'll join you for a short while,' she said, taking a seat next to him.

He poured a tequila in the glass she brought.

'*Santé*,' he said.

She sipped her tequila. 'You're a stranger in these parts,' she observed.

'If there are more pretty young women like you, I might be tempted to stay,' he said, with a smile.

'Most of us are already spoken for,' she replied.

'Your boyfriend is a lucky person,' he observed, drinking his tequila.

Was he toying with her? If he was, two could play that game.

'He's away at the moment,' she stated.

'That's good news,' he said. 'The last thing I needed was a jealous boyfriend to come bursting in here while you're having a social drink with me.'

'I take it that you haven't a girlfriend of your own,' suggested Maria.

'She's a long way away,' replied the other.

'By the way, I don't know your name,' said Maria.

'My name's Luis. What's yours?'

'Maria.'

'You don't run this place on you own, do you,

Maria?' said Luis, glancing around.

'My brother helps me to run it. But he only comes in after siesta time.' She realized that he was finding more out about her than she was about him.

'Will you be staying long in Verde?' she ventured.

'Long enough, I would think,' he replied enigmatically. He poured himself another drink and went to pour another for her. She put her hand over her glass.

'I've had enough already,' she protested.

'A pity,' he observed. 'Just when I thought we were going to be friends.'

'Well, maybe just one more.' If it meant that she would be able to find out anything else about him it would be worth having another tequila.

'I expect you've travelled around quite a bit,' she probed.

'Yes, I've been here and there,' he replied with a thin smile.

The last statement confirmed what she had already guessed. He was toying with her. He had no intention of revealing anything about his life or his past. The realization made her angry. She picked up her glass of tequila and emptied it in one gulp.

'Do you want another?' he demanded.

She stood up. 'No, I've got work to do. Thanks for the drinks,' she added, automatically.

'It's been my pleasure,' he said. 'Do you think I could have my hat and coat now?'

'I'll fetch them for you,' she replied. She was suddenly anxious to get rid of him. The fact that he had been toying with her now made her feel uncomfortable.

She went into the kitchen. She collected his hat and coat from the chair. To her surprise she found that he had followed her.

'Here you are,' she said, hastily thrusting the garments at him.

He accepted them calmly. His next action however took her completely by surprise. Instead of putting them on, he tossed them back on to the chair.

'What are you doing?' she demanded, with panic in her voice.

'You seem a nice friendly young woman,' he said. 'Let's see exactly how friendly you can become.'

So saying he seized her in a bear-like grip and began kissing her.

CHAPTER 17

Scarne was playing cards with the other outlaws. Outside the rain showed no sign of abating. They were playing poker, a game which Scarne enjoyed when he had the opportunity to play it.

They had been playing for about an hour and so far nobody had made any considerable gains. Scarne knew that the first thing to do when playing poker was to assess the opposition. He had been content to bide his time while he studied the faces around him and their reactions to each hand.

Since the contest would have been uneven with Manley having several hundred dollars after the robbery in San Caldiz, and the others having only a few dollars, Manley had given each of them fifty dollars.

'That's so we all start off equal,' he had stated.

'I'll take mine and go back to Verde to find a beautiful woman,' quipped Leguin.

'You'll stay here and play cards with us,' growled Manley.

'There's one thing missing,' said Lewis.

'What's that?' demanded Keeson.

'Some wine,' said Lewis. 'Cards and wine go together like . . .'

'Women and wine,' suggested Leguin.

'All right, let's get on with it,' said Manley.

Scarne early formed the impression that the player to watch out for was Garby. Normally he had very little to contribute to conversations. Scarne decided that he was a cut above the others in the intellectual field. He was probably better than the others when it came to playing poker.

The other three players seemed on a par. They all revealed that they had a good hand by a slight smile, or by some mannerism or other. Manley would stroke his chin thoughtfully – this was a sure indication that he had drawn cards which had improved his hand considerably. Lewis would try to conceal his excitement at having received good cards by covering his mouth with his hand. Leguin, whose mind seemed only half on the game in hand, would smile openly.

They had been playing for a further half an hour when Scarne received the hand he had been waiting for. He had been dealt two pairs; a pair of aces and a pair of jacks. On its own it would have been a hand worth raising the stakes for. But when he drew another ace he knew that here was a hand worth going all the way for. It was a full house, the next hand below four of a kind.

He was careful not to show the slightest flicker of emotion as he received the jack. He knew that Lewis was watching him like a hawk. The others had drawn two or three cards which obviously hadn't improved their hands to any great extent. Leguin and Keeson threw in their cards in disgust. Manley had drawn two cards, and after briefly assessing them he had announced that he was in and tossed a dollar into the pot.

Lewis, like Scarne, had drawn one card. He had shown no sign of emotion. He tossed a dollar into the pot. Scarne did the same.

The two who had dropped out watched with interest as the stakes increased. When it came that he would have to put in ten dollars to stay in the game, Manley dropped out. There was only Scarne and Lewis left.

Scarne watched Lewis for any slight sign as to the value of his hand. The stakes went higher and higher. Soon there was a hundred dollars in the pot. It was easily the biggest pot of the morning. Suddenly Scarne's close watch on Lewis was rewarded. When Lewis had collected his one card he had casually put it to the side of his other cards. Now he made a fatal error. He took hold of the card and placed it in the middle of the other cards. This could only mean that he had put it in sequence in his hand. Probably he had a run.

Which meant that Scarne had nothing to fear.

'I'll raise you a hundred dollars,' said Scarne.

The proverbial pin could have dropped from a great height and they would have heard it.

Lewis stared in disbelief at Scarne. The others held their breaths. After an eternity Lewis said, 'I'll see you.' He put a hundred dollars into the pot.

Scarne opened his hand out showing the full house. Lewis showed his run. There were whistles of appreciation from the others. It had been an exciting hand. Scarne collected the money.

'For that you can go into Verde and get some wine,' said Manley.

'And don't stay too long with that beautiful woman of yours,' added Leguin.

CHAPTER 18

In the kitchen Maria was struggling with Luis. He had succeeded in pushing her against one of the bare walls. He was holding her there with one arm across her face while he was fumbling under her frock with the other.

'Come on, my beauty,' he hissed. 'You know you want it.'

'If you hurt me, my boyfriend, Scarne, will kill you.'

She bit his arm, which had been covering her mouth. He didn't flinch.

'I've always liked a wild cat,' he growled.

Maria struggled to get underneath the arm which was pinning her against the wall. She managed to move a few inches lower, but his arm still anchored. With his other hand he managed to rip her underclothes. She could feel his hand fumbling against her bare flesh.

She bit his arm again. There was still no reaction. She desperately tried to slide down the wall. This time she managed to move a few more inches. In the excitement of searching between her legs, Luis loosened his grip on her face. She found that she was able to speak.

'Let me go and I'll give you some money,' she pleaded.

'I'm going to help myself to the money when I've finished with you.'

He was trying to prise open her legs but so far she had managed to prevent him.

'I'll report you to the other policemen,' she said, through clenched teeth.

'What policemen?' He paused for a moment.

'You're a policeman, aren't you?'

Luis chuckled. 'Me a policeman? The only time I've ever seen policemen is on the other side of my cell.'

'Then you're an outlaw,' she gasped.

'You've got it. Now if you'll keep still I'll give you something else.'

Having taken his arm from her face Luis now used his two hands to good effect. He pulled her down to the kitchen floor.

Maria gave a scream at the sudden change of tactic. She landed heavily on the floor, having first hit her head against the wall on the way down. She was momentarily dazed.

When the haze cleared in front of her eyes she realized with sudden horror that she was almost

completely naked. Luis had taken advantage of
her temporary blackout to rip off all her clothes.
He was lying on top of her. The only thing that had
saved her up to that moment was the fact that Luis
was having difficulty in divesting himself of his
trousers.

The realization that Luis was so close to gaining
his objective seemed to give her strength. She tried
to wriggle from underneath him.

'Keep still, you vixen,' he growled, hitting her in
the face with his clenched fist.

The blow only served to increase her efforts to
move from under him. She actually succeeded in
moving a couple of feet away from him. He
followed her. He hit her in the face again.

'For the last time, keep still,' he half shouted.

He was again lying on top of her. His trousers
stubbornly refused to slip over his boots. He tried
to kick them free. It was then that Maria spotted a
ghost of a chance to release herself from his grip.
Their movement on the floor had brought them
up against the fireplace. While Luis was fumbling
with his trousers he momentarily took his eyes off
Maria. Now was her chance. She knew exactly what
she had to do. A slight hesitation and her one
chance would be gone for ever.

In one swift movement she stretched upwards.
She grabbed the poker out of the fire. Luis's startled eyes suddenly registered her intention. But his
reaction was too late. Maria brought the poker

down swiftly and with deadly accuracy across his face. Luis's scream was far louder than Maria's had been.

When Scarne arrived at the cantina half an hour later Maria was sitting in the kitchen. She hadn't bothered to dress. She had just wrapped a blanket around herself.

'The front door was open,' Scarne began, then realized that something was terribly wrong. 'What is it? What's the matter?' he demanded with alarm.

'That bastard tried to rape me,' snapped Maria.

'Who?'

'The one I was telling you about. The one I thought was a policeman.'

'He wasn't a policeman, then?'

'He was an outlaw. The same as your friends,' she said, bitterly.

'You said he *tried* to rape you. . . ?'

'That's right. I hit him with this.' She pointed to the poker which was now lying outside the grate. It had cooled off.

'What happened then?'

'He ran off. He put a wet towel against his face.'

'You hit him with a hot poker,' stated Scarne, with sudden realization.

'That's right. The poker was in the fire. I pulled it out and hit him across the face,' said Maria, viciously.

'Never mind, it's all over now,' said Scarne,

102

trying to put his arms around her.

She pushed him away. 'Don't touch me. I don't ever want a man to touch me again.' She was beginning to get hysterical.

Scarne was surprised by her outburst but managed to keep a calm exterior.

'You've had a shock. Why don't you go and lie down. Have you got any laudanum?'

'I've got to fetch Juan,' she said, dully. 'He's at my brother's.'

'I'll go and tell him you're not well. I'll ask him if he can keep the boy for another few hours.'

'Don't tell him I've almost been raped,' pleaded Maria. 'I don't want anyone else to know.'

Scarne went out. It was still raining heavily. Scarne knew where Stephano lived and rode there quickly. He knocked at the cottage door.

Stephano scowled when he saw who the visitor was. He had never thought that Scarne was a suitable suitor for his sister.

Scarne explained that Maria wasn't feeling well and that she had gone to bed. Stephano agreed to look after Juan for the night.

'He often stays here all night,' he added.

When Scarne returned to the cantina he found that Maria had indeed gone to bed. She was lying in her bed facing the wall and with her back to him.

'I'll mix you some laudanum,' said Scarne. 'Where is it?'

103

'In the kitchen. In the table drawer,' she replied, tonelessly.

He found it and mixed her a stiff measure. He returned to the bedroom.

'Before you drink this I want you to answer a few questions.'

'I've had enough of questions,' she snapped.

'Did this guy – Luis – say where he was staying?'

'He said he was staying in a tent.'

'An outlaw staying in a tent,' said Scarne, thoughtfully.

'What difference does that make?' asked Maria, still with her back to him.

'It means in the first place that there are more than one of them. Outlaws don't come to Verde on their own. It also means that he and his friends have probably come after the gold.'

'Everything comes back to the gold, doesn't it,' she said, wearily.

'Don't you worry about it,' said Scarne. 'Here, drink the laudanum.'

She turned to face him. She accepted the drink. When she had finished it, she suddenly exclaimed. 'What if Luis comes back?'

'It's all right. I'll be staying here the night. Downstairs in the kitchen,' he added.

For the first time her attitude thawed. She even managed a smile. 'Thanks, Scarne,' she said. In a couple of minutes she was asleep.

Scarne took up his position in the kitchen after

making sure that the front and back doors were bolted. Would Luis come back this evening? The chances were against it. If Maria had hit him across the face with the hot poker as she described, the chances were that it would take him a few days to recover from the pain. The chances were that, whenever that might be, that would be the time he would be coming back to seek revenge on Maria.

CHAPTER 19

Scarne rode slowly back to the mine. His thoughts were focused on the events of the past day. He had spent the night in the chair in the kitchen with a gun by his side. It had only been a precaution since he had guessed that it would take Luis a few days before he ventured back to the scene where he had received a hot poker across his face.

There was no doubt though that one day Luis would be back to seek his revenge. So before he had set out Scarne had insisted that Maria should close the cantina and go to stay with her brother. Scarne had helped her to carry her belongings to her brother's house. When he had arrived there Juan's face had lit up. He had gone to fetch the ball which they had played with before. Scarne had spent a few minutes with him as they had tossed the ball back and forth.

Maria had finally settled in. There was an

awkward moment when Scarne was about to leave them. He picked Juan up and gave him a hug. Maria stared up at Scarne with large troubled eyes.

'Will everything be all right?' she demanded.

'It will be all right, I promise,' he said, kissing her lightly on the lips.

As he rode back to the mine he wondered grimly whether he would be able to keep that promise.

Manley greeted him with the customary scowl. 'Where the hell have you been?' he demanded.

'Finding out about another gang of outlaws who are not too far away,' replied Scarne.

Manley's expression changed to one of concern. The others gathered around Scarne. He explained how an outlaw named Luis had attacked Maria, but how she had managed to defend herself.

'The lady has courage,' supplied Leguin.

'Never mind about that,' snapped Manley. 'The question is what are we going to do about it?'

'We have to assume that Luis did not come to Verde on his own,' stated Scarne. 'There must be a gang out there somewhere.'

'The thing to do is to attack them before they attack us,' said Keeson.

'First of all we have to find out where they are camping,' said Scarne. 'I suggest I try to find

108

them. I know the land around here better than any of you. I would guess they are camping to the east of the town – somewhere not too far away.'

'Yeah, that sounds reasonable,' said Manley. 'If you can find out how many there are we can decide whether to attack them.'

'Perhaps they're not after the gold,' suggested Lewis. 'In which case the whole exercise would be a waste of time.'

'Of course they're after the gold,' snapped Manley. 'No one would come to this god-forsaken town unless they were after the gold.'

'My guess is that they have camped at the same spot where we stopped the night before we came into Verde,' said Scarne. 'It's a good place for a camp with plenty of shelter and running water.'

'Take care,' said Manley. 'We wouldn't want to lose you. If we did we wouldn't be able to start working on the mine.'

Scarne glanced at the Mexicans. The rain had stopped and the Mexicans were now busy clearing the entrance to the mine. 'It'll take them a day or so before we'll be ready to start work,' said Scarne.

'When are you going to start?' demanded Manley.

'Now is as good a time as any,' said Scarne.

He set off aiming to skirt the town. The rain had

109

given way to lowering clouds and there was a fresh breeze blowing. As he rode along he thought of Maria's suggestion that the three of them could go to Topez. Manley and the others wouldn't be able to follow them there, since they wouldn't know where they were. He had a couple of days before Manley would expect him back at the mine. If he changed direction and rode into Verde he could pick up Maria and Juan.

It was a tempting idea. It would mean forgetting about the mine. But as Maria had pointed out, when they did succeed in getting the gold out there was bound to be bloodshed. And the chances were that some of that blood could be his.

Why then didn't he change direction now and ride into Verde? If he were perfectly honest the only thing that kept him from doing so was the four-letter word – gold. His grandfather had spent all his life searching for gold. He had arrived too late at the goldfield and had ended up with only a few meagre nuggets. But when he was a boy he had listened avidly to his grandfather's stories of the miners who had made a fortune when they had spotted the elusive yellow substance in a river, or as nuggets in a mine. The stories had fired his imagination. He had resolved that when he became a man, at the first opportunity he would try to work in a gold-mine. The opportunity had arisen with Fernando's mine. Of course it hadn't worked out. But now he was having a second chance to find the elusive gold. And he was determined to go for it. No matter how tempting Maria's suggestion was that the three of them could escape to Topez.

CHAPTER 20

Scarne was riding through rugged country. He guessed he had passed Topez on his right and would now be heading towards the outlaws' camp. The mountains that stretched away to the east formed a natural barrier and it was unlikely that the outlaws would have set up their camp on its slopes. The mountains did, however, provide him with fresh water from its streams and both he and his horse availed themselves of it from time to time.

He was careful to choose his route so that he rode through gullies whenever he could. It often meant taking detours, but even if the outlaws hadn't posted a look-out, he still didn't want to take that chance. He knew that it was vital that he spotted them before they saw him.

The day was drawing to a close. He knew he would have to find a sheltered spot soon to pitch his tent. The terrain had changed and he was now riding through trees and thickets. He found a clearing among some willow trees and dismounted. He decided that it would be a suitable place to spend the night. He was about to unroll his blanket when he received an unexpected shock. He could hear voices.

He stood stock still and placed his hand over his horse's muzzle. The voices came closer. He distinguished that there were two men. He guessed he had stumbled across the outlaws.

The two men were obviously on foot. This gave him a slight advantage, since if they discovered his whereabouts he would be able to jump on his horse and high-tail it out of the trees. In the growing darkness he should be able to make his escape.

The other thing he learned from their being on foot was that their camp was nearby. This was confirmed when he heard one of them say, 'We might as well call it a day and go back to the camp. We're not going to catch anything now.'

'But I'm sure I saw an antelope come into these trees,' said the other.

'Even if you did it's too dark now to find it. We'll try again in the morning.'

'Think of it,' said the other, and their voices began to fade as they walked away. 'Real meat for a change.'

Scarne smiled. The conversation could almost have been a copy of the one the other outlaws held a few days before. He waited until the sounds of

114

them going away had disappeared. He finished unrolling his blanket. He munched the usual dry biscuit which made up his supper. Before turning in he reminded himself that he would have to be up at the crack of dawn. He knew that the thought would be enough to awake him.

Sure enough the first grey light was filtering from the east when he opened his eyes. He prodded his horse with his foot. He wanted the chestnut mare saddled and ready in case they had to beat a quick retreat.

After tying her to a convenient tree he set out in the direction the voices had come from on the previous night. He moved slowly and carefully, trying to make as little noise as possible. The light was now clear enough for him to see several yards ahead. Suddenly he saw a flash of movement. In a second it was gone. But he had seen enough to confirm that it had been an antelope. The two hunters had been right, he thought grimly.

The trees were giving him ideal cover as he slipped from one to the other. The question was whether he was going in the right direction. Maybe he had already passed the camp. He decided he had better stay where he was. The outlaws' camp would reveal itself shortly in the way all camps do.

In fact he stayed hiding behind a friendly tree for a considerable time before the outlaws did what he expected them to do. They lit a fire. The smell coming from the smoke told him in which direction they were camping. In fact he had over-shot their position. He was glad that he had not been tempted to go further ahead. Now he had to retrace his steps carefully.

The sounds of their voices now could be heard clearly. All he had to do was to establish how many outlaws there were. He peered carefully through the trees.

Sure enough they had camped in an open space not a hundred yards from where he was hiding. He counted five tents. That meant at least five men. On the other hand some of the tents could be sleeping two men. In which case he could increase their number.

This was confirmed when two men came out of the nearest tent. Scarne watched eagerly, waiting for the others to appear. Two more appeared from another tent. Then two more. In fact the final count was nine men since only one appeared from the far tent. Scarne guessed that he was the leader.

They were nine while the outlaws at the mine numbered five. Of course he would include himself with their number since, if it came to a shoot-out, he would have to throw in his lot with them.

The smell of beans cooking reminded him that he too was hungry. Well, there was nothing he could do about it now. He had better get back to the mine and report his findings. He was about to turn away when a sound stopped him.

It was the unmistakable sound of a horse whinnying. He knew instinctively that it was his chestnut mare. Even though she must have been about half a mile away she was making enough noise to wake the dead. As it was it certainly galvanized the men in front of him into action. They dived for their horses which were grazing nearby.

Scarne began to run. He knew that there was no point in trying to conceal his presence. His only chance was to reach his horse before the pursuers reached him. Judging from the sounds they were making as they crashed through the trees after him the chances of him getting to his horse were pretty slim.

He was running as he had never run for years. Men who spend most of their lives on horses are generally not fleet of foot. The truth of this statement was borne out as he gasped for air in his effort to outdistance his pursuers. He knew that they were still a short distance behind him. The fact that they had to ride through the trees was hindering their progress.

The one thing Scarne feared was that when one of them had a clear view of him they would open fire. The last thing he wanted was to suffer a bullet wound, or even die in this god-forsaken place. He made one final effort to reach his horse which he could now see ahead.

The fact that he was on the last lap gave Scarne added strength. He sped over the last hundred yards as quickly as the antelope would have done. He dived up on to his horse, unhitching her in the same movement.

Even as he rode through the trees he realized that the odds were stacked against him. The chestnut mare was not the quickest of horses and once he reached the open country his pursuers would soon catch him. As if to remind him that they were not far away, one of them fired at him.

The shot went wide, but it confirmed Scarne's belief that his prospect of reaching a ripe old age was decreasing by the minute. He desperately searched for a way of escaping from his situation. Another bullet winging past his ear confirmed that it was a matter of urgency.

The open country now couldn't be too far ahead. Scarne suddenly veered to the left. This took him back among the trees. He carried on for some distance until he was sure that the pursuers were following him. As he rode he searched for a particular kind of tree. It had to be an old tree with thick branches.

He finally came across one. He rode underneath the overhanging branch. He pulled up the horse underneath. He swung up on to the branch from the saddle. The horse stayed underneath the branch. Scarne fired a shot at its legs. It raced away as if its tail was on fire.

Scarne moved to a comfortable spot on the branch and waited for his pursuers. He did not have long to wait. The first of them rode underneath his hiding place as quickly as he could between the trees. Scarne who was only a couple of feet above him held his breath.

None of the riders looked up as they concentrated on following the sound of the chestnut mare which was crashing through the trees ahead. Scarne counted the riders as they passed underneath. Four . . . five . . . six . . . seven . . . eight. . . . Scarne waited for the last rider. He soon appeared. Scarne tensed as he watched him approaching the branch.

When the rider was directly underneath Scarne jumped. He landed on the rider's shoulders and his weight knocked the two of them to the ground. Scarne was the quicker to recover. He hit the rider on the head with his gun. It signified the end of his interest in the pursuit.

Scarne managed to catch the rider's horse. The others had ridden on ahead oblivious of the event. It would take them some time to catch the chestnut mare since, without a rider, she would be able to race as quickly as their horses. Scarne guessed that he would have enough time to disappear into the distance before the pursuers discovered their mistake. He was congratulating himself on pulling off a neat trick when there came the sound of an approaching horse. Scarne was so surprised that for once his reaction was slow. The new rider was already covering him with his gun before he could draw his.

'I think you'd better come back to the camp with me,' said the man with the gun.

CHAPTER 21

Half an hour later Scarne was in the outlaws' camp. The other riders who had been following his horse had returned too. The expressions of surprise on their faces would have amused Scarne if the situation hadn't been so deadly serious.

'So you're the guy who was watching the camp,' said the leader, who had been introduced as Hillman.

'No, you've got it wrong. I was just passing,' said Scarne.

Hillman was a stocky man with a short neck and a square, pockmarked face. 'Since you were just passing you'd better introduce yourself,' he said.

'My name's Stevens,' said Scarne, picking out the first name he could think of.

'Stevens,' said Hillman, thoughtfully. 'And you were just passing,' he echoed, just as thoughtfully.

It was obvious to Scarne that Hillman didn't believe him. But if he stuck to his story there wasn't much that Hillman could do about it.

'Nobody just passes this place,' said Hillman, meaningfully.

'I was on my way to Topez,' lied Scarne. 'I just wanted somewhere to camp for the night.'

'Topez,' stated Hillman.

It was beginning to get on Scarne's nerves the way Hillman was repeating everything. However he knew he had to keep cool.

'If you were an innocent traveller, as you say,' said Hillman, 'why did you run off like that?'

'Wouldn't you run off if you saw nine men chasing you,' said Scarne.

'Ten,' said the outlaw who had brought Scarne in.

'Connolly is always last,' supplied Hillman.

Scarne sighed. Connolly was a small man who was older than the others. If he had been with the rest of the riders he, Scarne, would be on his way to the mine now. Instead of which he was here, surrounded by outlaws who obviously didn't believe his story. He glanced around. One of them had an interesting scar on the side of his face. This must be Luis, the one who had attacked Maria. If he ever had a chance he'd give him more than a scar as a memento of the assault.

'We're not going to get anywhere with him,' announced Hillman, who had obviously come to a decision.

Scarne allowed himself a glimmer of some hope.

If they weren't going to get anything out of him then they could let him go, couldn't they?

Hillman's next statement scattered that hope to the winds. 'So we'll just have to shoot him.' To illustrate the point he drew his gun.

The other outlaws were staring interestedly at the confrontation. Scarne instinctively knew that he would get no help from them. Hillman drew back the hammer of his gun. Scarne knew that his life's expectancy was now measured in seconds. He closed his eyes. He wanted his last seconds to have a mental picture of Maria.

He pictured her face. They could have had a lovely future together. The two of them and young Juan. He should have followed her advice and taken them to Topez. They could have been happy there. Far away from the mine and all the trouble it had brought.

Hillman was taking a long time to pull the trigger. Scarne opened his eyes. Hillman was staring at him thoughtfully. 'Empty your pockets,' he growled.

'Here, I'll do it.' One of the outlaws stepped forward.

He dived into Scarne's pockets. He came out with the makings of cigarettes, a few dollars and some loose change, and a handkerchief.

'Is that all?' demanded Hillman.

'I travel light,' said Scarne.

Hillman picked up the handkerchief. It was a

large white handkerchief. It was distinctive since there was some embroidery in the corner. Too late Scarne realized what it was. It had been embroidered by Victoria when she had been staying at his cottage. It all seemed like a century ago. But the embroidery was real and belonged to the present. She had embroidered his name.

'I think you had better tell us the truth, Scarne,' said Hillman, moving his revolver closer to Scarne's head.

CHAPTER 22

On the mountain above the mine the Apaches were holding a council of war. Their leader, Lion Who Roars in the Night, was addressing the assembled braves. They were all squatting around him. There were seventeen in all.

'The time has come for action,' he said. There was a chorus of agreement. 'We've been very patient,' he announced. 'We've waited for twelve moons. Nobody could have been more patient than us.'

'Now is the time for action,' cried one of the braves. Again there was a chorus of agreement.

'The Mexican with the shifting eyes can no longer be trusted. He has promised us gold and up to now he has not brought us any.'

'He knows we cannot go into the mine because the bones of our ancestors are buried there,' said a brave.

'So he has been toying with us all these moons,'

said another. 'He has been pretending there is gold in the mine.'

'So we are all agreed that the time has come to kill the Mexican,' said the chief.

'Perhaps we should take a count on it,' suggested one of the braves. His name was Antelope Afraid of the Wind, and he was smaller than the rest of the braves.

'I don't see why we should take a count on it,' said the chief, threateningly.

'If we take a count we could smoke a pipe while we are counting,' suggested Antelope Afraid of the Wind, with a cunning smile.

The mood of the assembled braves changed imperceptibly. Most of them would secretly like to smoke a pipe. They hadn't smoked a pipe for weeks. They enjoyed the euphoria which a smoke brought. The actual ingredients of the concoction inside the pipe was known only to the medicine-man. Some of the braves, though, realized that he used some of the white poppies which grew in abundance in a field over a nearby hill.

'Well I suppose we might as well smoke a pipe while we're waiting for the counting to end,' said the chief.

The medicine-man set about mixing his concoction. Another brave was dispatched to collect the stones from the chief's tent so that they could make the count. Several of the braves rubbed their hands in eager anticipation of smoking the pipe.

'The Mexican said he was going to make us rich,' said one of the braves.

'All this time he has been in the mine and he hasn't brought us a single gold stone back.'

'Only those yellow stones which he brought us in the first place,' said one of the braves. 'He pretended to us that they were gold. But we knew better,' he ended proudly.

'It's what the Pale Faces call fool's gold,' supplied another.

'When the big American was here . . .' began the chief.

'Scarne,' supplied one of the braves.

'We knew we could trust him. If he said there was gold in the mine, then we could believe him.'

The pipe was produced and the stones placed in a leather pouch. The stones were round pebbles, either white or black. They had been used by the Apaches for generations to vote on matters of disagreement.

The braves stood in single file. The first one approached the chief, who handed him the bag. The brave searched inside for a suitable stone to indicate his wishes.

'White to kill the Mexican. Black to let him live,' intoned the chief.

The brave palmed the stone without showing the chief what colour it was. He then went over to another leather bag which the medicine-man was holding. The brave placed the stone inside the

127

bag, again so that it was not visible to the person holding it. The process was repeated until all the braves had deposited their stones. They then all gathered round in a circle while the medicine-man's bag was emptied. The stones were counted. There were four for letting the Mexican live. The thirteen for killing him won the vote.

'We'll kill him the next time he comes out of the mine,' announced the chief.

There was a cheer from the assembled braves.

CHAPTER 23

Scarne had been in some tricky situations in his life but the one in which he now found himself would have topped them all. Not only had Hillman's gun moved closer to his head but the outlaws had also moved closer. The wild idea occurred to Scarne that they had stepped nearer in order to have a better ringside seat at his killing.

'Your handkerchief says that your name is Scarne,' growled Hillman.

'It's somebody else's handkerchief. A guy gave it to me,' lied Scarne.

'Now why should a guy give another guy a hand-kerchief?' demanded Hillman. 'Unless you're like that.' He gave the limp hand sign which was universally recognized.

'If this guy is Scarne, the one who owns the mine, it could save us a lot of trouble,' said one of the outlaws.

'I'll soon find out if his name is Scarne or not,'

said Luis, threateningly. 'If his name is Scarne I owe him for what his girlfriend did to me.' He indicated the purple scar on his face.

Why didn't he admit who he really was? The question had kept flashing through his mind like one of the newfangled magic lanterns. As soon as the question arose he brushed it to one side. Once he had admitted he was Scarne these outlaws would have an unshakable hold on those working at the mine. They could hold him as a hostage. Since he was the only one who could work the mine the outlaws who were now staring at him with undisguised hostility would hold all the trump cards.

Another reason for not telling them his real identity was that they could force him to lead them to the mine. Since these were comparative newcomers it was reasonable to assume that they did not know the exact whereabouts of the mine. If he had to lead them there they would then be in a position to ambush Manley and company. Not that he would have had any regrets about seeing them killed. But the outlaws you know are better than the outlaws you don't know. He smiled grimly at the thought.

'You've got one last chance,' snarled Hillman. 'Are you Scarne?'

'No,' replied Scarne. 'I've told you. My name is Stevens.'

'Let me get the truth out of him,' said Luis.

At a sign from Hillman two outlaws stepped forward and tied Scarne's hands behind his back. Luis had stripped to the waist revealing a well-muscled body. On his face there was a smile of satisfaction.

'I'm going to have this scar that your girlfriend gave me for the rest of my life,' he said. 'But I'll give you something to remember as well.'

He aimed to punch Scarne around the body. Scarne moved away from the first few blows. But with his hands tied behind his back he knew that it would only be a short time before the blows started to land. The outlaws shouted their encouragement to Luis. Even Hillman permitted himself a thin smile at the contest.

Luis's lips were bared in a wolflike grin. Although only a couple of his blows had landed up until that moment he knew that it was only a matter of time before he caught up with the danc-ing American. In fact a couple of moments later one of his blows did land. Scarne instinctively winced, although he tried not to show that he had been hurt.

Luis stalked him like a fox after his prey. Scarne tried to sidestep another of Luis's blows but the result was it caught him in the kidneys. Scarne could not prevent the groan of pain which escaped from his lips. The outlaws howled with glee at his reaction.

More and more of Luis's body blows were land-

131

ing. Scarne knew that his movements were becoming sluggish. Once he tried to kick Luis, but the effort of trying to do so with his hands tied behind his back almost sent him sprawling. Luis's smile widened. He even walked round Scarne without delivering a blow to show that he was completely in charge. The outlaws were yelling their heads off – pleading with him to go in for the kill.

Scarne knew that he could not keep up shuffling around much longer. Luis was now landing blow after blow. He almost wished that Luis would land one final blow to finish him off. His body was aching excruciatingly. It was at that moment that he decided on one last fling. When the idea came to him a smile brushed his lips.

Luis spotted Scarne's change of expression. He hesitated although the outlaws were still baying for blood. Scarne stared contemptuously at Luis's face. The scar which Maria had given him had seemed to change colour while they were fighting and had now assumed a purple colour.

Luis had decided that the thin smile on Scarne's lips didn't signify anything. He stepped inside preparing to deliver a final blow. To Luis's surprise he never delivered it, since Scarne fell on the ground.

'Get up,' snarled Luis.

'Go on. Get up,' echoed the outlaws, sensing that the fight was not yet over.

Scarne judged his distance. He knew he would

only have one chance. Luis was waiting for him to make a move. When it came he was completely unprepared. Scarne kicked upwards and his boot landed between Luis's legs.

Luis's howl of pain gave Scarne massive satisfaction. However it was destined to be short-lived. An outlaw stepped behind him and clubbed him on the head with his gun. This time Scarne was indeed out for the count.

CHAPTER 24

Outside the mine Manley and company were engaged in a heated debate.

'What are we going to do now?' demanded Lewis.

The five surveyed the entrance to the mine. The Mexicans had finished clearing it an hour before. They had been paid off and they had all gone home.

'We are ready to start working the mine,' supplied Keeson.

'I would have thought that's obvious,' snapped Manley.

'We're ready to start working the mine and now we can't go ahead because Scarne isn't here,' complained Leguin.

'We should never have let him go,' stated Lewis, flatly.

'Well he's gone and that's that.' Manley spat the words out.

'We could sit around here for days, waiting for him to come back,' said Garby, who normally didn't have much to say.

'Where did he think the outlaws might have camped?' asked Lewis.

'Somewhere near the spot where we camped the night before we came into Verde,' explained Manley, having recovered his composure.

'He went the day before yesterday,' said Lewis, thoughtfully. 'He should have got there before nightfall. Yesterday he should have found out exactly where they had camped. He would still have had time to get back here before nightfall. Now it's past midday.'

'Something might have happened to him,' suggested Leguin.

The others looked at each other with dismay.

'If so it means that all this work is for nothing,' said Lewis.

They looked towards Manley for guidance.

'There's nothing much we can do today,' he said, slowly. 'But we'll set off first thing in the morning to find Scarne.'

There was a muted chorus of agreement.

In Verde the topic of conversation was the closure of Maria's cantina. A small crowd was standing around, staring at it with disbelieving eyes.

'It's never closed before,' said one regular customer.

'When Maria's father was alive he even kept it open when they appointed a new pope,' said another.

'Maria always kept it so spotless,' opined another. 'Not like some of the other cantina owners I could mention.'

'Somebody said that Maria was attacked,' said an old gossip who could generally be depended upon to come up with the latest morsel of tittle-tattle.

There was a stunned silence.

'Maria? Attacked?' demanded another.

'That's what I heard.'

'Not by somebody in the town?'

'Oh, no. I heard it was a stranger.'

They looked around as thought half-expecting to see the stranger nearby. But the only man they failed to recognize was a small man who didn't look as though he would harm a fly.

'So where is Maria now?' demanded one of the crowd.

'They say she's staying with her brother,' came the reply.

'The one who lives in David Street,' supplied another.

The small man slipped away unnoticed. David Street, he should be able to find that. He began to scan the names of the streets as he walked slowly past.

Yes, there it was. A dozen or so houses set back from the main street. There were a few children playing outside the houses. He approached one of the older boys and asked him where Maria, who owned the cantina was staying. The boy jerked a thumb in the direction of one of the houses.

Connolly approached it. He hesitated before knocking at the door. A stunning Mexican opened it. From Luis's description, Connolly had no difficulty in recognizing her as Maria.

'You are Maria?'

She confirmed it with a nod.

'You must come quickly. Scarne is hurt.' This part was quite true since nobody survives being hit hard with the butt of a gun without feeling pain.

Maria's eyes widened. 'He sent you a message?'

'Yes. You mustn't tell anyone.'

'I've got to tell my brother,' she gasped. 'He's looking after my son.'

'All right. Nobody else. And hurry.'

Maria found Stephano. She explained to him that Scarne had been hurt and that she was going to the mine. Stephano put his head outside the door. Any fears he might have had that the whole thing was a trick was dispelled when he saw the small man standing there.

'We've got to hurry,' said Connolly.

Stephano fetched Maria's horse. She hesitated.

'What now?' demanded Connolly.

'I want to give my son a kiss,' said Maria.

Connolly tried to conceal his exasperation while Maria disappeared back inside the house. However she appeared in a few moments. 'He's asleep,' she explained.

They set off in the direction of the mine. However they were barely out of sight of the town when Connolly veered sharply to the right.

'Where are you going?' demanded Maria, with alarm.

'I told you I'm taking you to see Scarne,' replied Connolly. 'But he's not at the mine.'

Any thoughts Maria had held about arguing with him were quickly dispelled when she saw the gun he was holding.

CHAPTER 25

The Mexican stepped out into the daylight. He had spent the usual day in the mine searching for gold-nuggets. The mine consisted of a labyrinth of caves and he had spent the past two years searching them. The result had always been the same – he had been unable to find any traces of gold.

The Indians met him with blank stares. This was nothing new, since their faces rarely showed any signs of emotion.

'No gold,' he intoned, in what had become his customary statement when he stepped out of the mine.

They nodded silently. Was there something different about their attitude? His eyes raked them as he tried to guess what it was. All the braves seemed to be there. Which was unusual in itself, since he was normally met by at the most half a dozen.

Suddenly fear began to grip him. Their

combined stares were unnerving him. He knew that coming out of the mine month after month with the same shake of his head had meant that his credentials as a gold-finder were non-existent. The question had been how long he could keep from explaining to the Apaches that he had found nothing.

No longer, it seemed. They moved inexorably towards him. He wished he had learned to speak their language so that he could explain to them that the chances of finding gold were about a million to one. But he had never bothered to learn their language. He had been too lazy. He had depended on the few words of English that some of the Apaches knew and, of course, sign language.

Now was the time to use sign language as he had never used it before. The trouble was, what signs did he use to say that the whole venture had become impossible? He had realized it months ago. But he had kept going, partly because the Apaches had expected him to keep going.

In addition they fed him. They had even provided him with a young squaw to keep him company in his bed at night. He had the impression that she had been persuaded to come to him because none of the braves had wanted her as their wife, since she was dumb. But she had been his companion for nearly two years. Now apparently it was all over.

The braves moved closer. It didn't escape the

Mexican's notice that they all wore their knives in their belts. Normally they didn't carry their knives unless they were going hunting. His mouth became unbearably dry as he realized that that was exactly what they were doing. They had a prey. Himself.

Suddenly their inexorable progress was brought to a halt by an unexpected arrival. It was his squaw. She dived between the advancing braves and himself. She held up her hand in a universal gesture that meant halt.

She made a gesture across her throat, which was also universally recognized as someone cutting somebody else's throat. The braves had stopped their progress. But now they were obviously getting restless. One or two advanced surreptitiously.

The squaw made one final gesture. She pointed to her belly. She made a gesture signifying that it would get bigger. She held up seven fingers, signifying that in seven moons something drastic was going to happen. It did not require any more signs to explain what that something was going to be.

A few of the braves hesitated. This was something they had not bargained for. If the squaw, whose name was Silent as the Wind, was pregnant then the Mexican would become their blood-brother. Apache law stated that they couldn't kill their blood-brother with a simple count of the stones. There had to be a full meeting of all the council. This meant including the women. And they would never agree to killing the husband of someone who was expecting a baby.

The braves began to depart. None of them glanced at the Mexican as they did so. He took hold of Silent as the Wind's hand. He knew he would be eternally grateful to her for saving his life. Maybe he should play a bigger part in the life of the community. One thing he resolved for sure – he would learn their language.

CHAPTER 26

Another confrontation was taking place where a woman was the centre-piece. This was in the outlaws' camp. Connolly had brought Maria to the camp. She had protested vociferously for much of the way. Finally Connolly had threatened to hit her with his revolver if she didn't shut up. She had obeyed his instruction.

When they reached the camp she had still been puzzled as to why she had been brought there. There were a few men sitting around. It didn't take her experience in the cantina to identify them as outlaws. When she dismounted, one of them, a stocky man with a pockmarked face approached her.

'I'm Hillman. I'm their leader.' He waved a hand to indicate the men who were sitting around.

'I demand to know why I've been brought here,' said Maria, indignantly.

'All in good time,' said Hillman. He gestured to

one of the bandits who went inside one of the tents. When he came out he was accompanied by a person whom Maria instantly recognized.

'You!' she gasped.

Luis stepped up to her. He stopped in front of her. He seemed to be having some difficulty in walking.

'We've got some unfinished business,' he hissed.

'Never mind about that,' snapped Hillman. 'Is she the person you were talking about?'

'Of course she is,' snarled Luis. He turned and hobbled back to the tent.

'Right, bring the other one,' commanded Hillman.

The messenger disappeared inside another tent. When he reappeared he brought out another familiar figure.

'Scarne,' gasped Maria.

'That's all we wanted to know,' said Hillman, with a satisfied smile.

'Something has happened to him,' stated Keeson.

'I would have thought that's bloody obvious,' snarled Manley.

'There's no point in hanging around here any longer,' said Lewis. 'We'll have to go after him.'

'All right,' said Manley, coming to a decision. 'Check your guns.'

They were thumbing ammunition into their revolvers when Leguin stated:

'I'm beginning to wish we hadn't come to this place. We've been hanging around here for days. Now, when at last we have a chance to start finding gold, we can't do anything because our leader has disappeared.'

'I'm your leader, and don't forget it,' snapped Manley.

Leguin gave a gallic shrug.

They mounted their horses. As if by consent they all glanced at the mine. Then they turned and began to ride forward, Indian style, with Manley leading.

They knew the journey in front of them was going to take several hours. They didn't waste any energy talking. Each one was too busy with his own thoughts.

Manley was thinking of a life of ease, of a time when he had amassed enough gold. He would buy a ranch in some state other than Texas – a state where he was not wanted for murder and robbery. He would have a manager to run the ranch and servants to wait on him. He would be lord of all he surveyed. He would open a box of the best cigars each morning. No, his servant would open the box for him. During the day he would always have a glass of Napoleon brandy by his side. He would be living in a large ranch where he would entertain other guests from time to time – other gentry, of course. He would make substantial donations towards the local school and church. Who knows, that might even make him mayor of the town. He half-smiled at the thought.

Keeson had decided he would open a gambling casino with the money from his share of the gold. He had heard that San Francisco was becoming known as Sin City. That would be the place for him. He would open a casino. Or maybe two or three, depending on how much money he would have when they had finished mining. He would wear silk shirts and wear trousers with gold braid. He would walk among the gaming-tables and everyone would glance at him with respect. He would smoke those scented cigarettes and drink wine out of one those long glasses. Everyone would envy him. He would be the toast of San Francisco.

Lewis knew that when he had the money he would be able to realize his life-long ambition – he would become a banker. He would start off in a small way by buying a bank. Then later, once he had established himself, he would branch out into neighbouring towns. He would visit his branches in a carriage drawn by four grey horses. His carriage would be a familiar sight in the locality. He would marry a woman from one of the old established families. The marriage would be the social event of the year. They would have several children. He had always imagined that it would be pleasant to spend time playing with his own children. Not in the way his father had treated him by beating him regularly.

Garby knew exactly what part of the world he would go to when he received his share of the money – Kentucky. There, he would breed horses. He had always loved horses. It had always been his ambition to own race-horses. Now he would have the chance. He would enter them in the local races. Of course the ultimate thrill would be in entering them and winning the Kentucky Derby. He might even consider going over to England where the original Derby was held. They knew everything about horses in England. Maybe he could even buy some horses from over there, and bring them back here. His day-dream had caused him to fall slightly behind the others. He gave his horse a kick to get him to catch up with the others.

Leguin had been nursing his day-dream for ages. It simply meant going back to France. To Paris, to be exact. He wouldn't be able to get back there quick enough. He had come to America to make his fortune. He would make his fortune in the mine. *Et, voilá*, he would return to France and spend it.

America was not the country for him. For one thing he was not able to get champagne. *Sacré bleu!* Most of all he was homesick. He missed the hustle and bustle of Paris. Oh, he knew that some said he should go to St Louis, where he would feel at home, since hundreds of Frenchmen had settled there. But it would never approach Paris. It would never approach the most beautiful city in the world with Montmartre, the *Tour Eiffel,* and the Seine running though it. He blinked a tear away just thinking about it.

They had ridden for a few hours. The terrain was now changing. They were riding through rugged undulating country where there were winding gullies, evidence of river-beds which had long since dried out. When they were in one of them it meant that they couldn't see over the top. They could only see what lay ahead. When they went round one of the bends they could indeed see quite clearly what did lie ahead. It was a group of men riding towards them. In the lead was Scarne and they weren't out for a pleasure ride, since the rider who was accompanying him was holding a pistol to Scarne's head.

CHAPTER 27

The two parties stared at each other for a moment in stunned surprise. Scarne was the first to recover. He grabbed the pistol from the hands of the rider who was by his side. They had not bothered to tie his hands, thinking that to truss up Maria, who was riding in the rear, would be enough.

There was a brief struggle, but the outlaw was no match for Scarne. He twisted the revolver out of the other's grip. He turned it on the outlaw and shot him. It was the signal for all hell to break loose.

The outlaws dived for their guns. Scarne, since he already had a gun in his hand, shot at two of the outlaws who were accompanying him. He managed to kill one, but the other escaped due to his horse panicking and racing off.

Both groups of riders were now firing indiscriminately at each other. Scarne saw one of his band of outlaws fall, but his main concern was for Maria. He rode heedlessly through the gunfire towards the back of the column. There, Hillman was guarding Maria. Scarne was about fifty yards away from them when Hillman swung Maria from her saddle and placed her on his horse as a shield.

'If you come any closer, Scarne, I'll kill her,' he shouted above the noise of the gunfire.

'Kill him, Scarne,' screamed Maria. 'Never mind about me.'

'Drop your gun, Scarne, or I'll kill her,' yelled Hillman.

Scarne knew that he had no choice. He tossed his gun to the ground. The smile of triumph on Hillman's face was nauseating to see.

However, it was short-lived. Hillman was holding his gun to Maria's head. Suddenly his horse, frightened by the proximity of the gunfire, reared. Maria seized her opportunity. She pushed Hillman out of the saddle. They both fell to the ground.

Both men had lost their guns somewhere in the undergrowth. They stood up at the same time. Hillman looked around for a possible chance of escape. There was none. Most of his gang were either dead or dying.

'It's just you and me, Hillman,' said Scarne.

Hillman realized the truth of the statement with

growing dread. He knew he stood no chance against Scarne. He backed away. There were rider-less horses milling around. Hillman thought he had spotted his chance. He grabbed one of the horses. Even as he did so, Scarne grabbed him. He pulled Hillman away from the horse, which galloped away.

'As I said, it's just you and me, Hillman,' said Scarne.

Hillman knew that he had no choice but to stand and fight. He tried one of the oldest tricks in the book. He feigned to slip when Scarne advanced. As Hillman went down he grabbed a handful of dirt. He tried to throw it in the eyes of the advancing Scarne. But he was not successful. Scarne blinked the dust away.

He began to hit Hillman. All the humiliation he and Maria had suffered during the past hours went into the body blows. Hillman tried ineffectually to block them. The strength of Scarne's blows forced Hillman to his knees. Scarne scornfully dragged him upright. He began to hit him in the face. Hillman shook his head to try to avoid the blows, but without success. His face was soon a mass of blood.

Scarne was vaguely aware that the sound of gunfire had ceased. He took a moment to glance up at the result of the gun-battle. He was shocked to discover that there only appeared to be two persons left riding on a horse: Leguin and Manley.

Scarne was so startled at the discovery that he

completely took his gaze from Hillman. The outlaw made one last desperate effort to escape. He had spotted his gun in the undergrowth. He dived towards it. He was about to pick it up when Manley shot him, blowing his brains out.

'Thanks,' said Scarne.

After confirming that Lewis, Keeson and Garby were indeed dead, the three started back for the mine. Maria had enquired about burying them. Manley had pointed out that they didn't have any spades. Anyhow, the circling vultures would soon save them the work.

The four rode in silence. It was late in the after-noon when they reached the mine. There was nobody in sight.

They dismounted.

'I suppose we can always get some workers from the town to help us,' suggested Manley.

'Yeah, that might be possible,' Scarne agreed.

'It will take longer, won't it?' asked Leguin.

'It will take longer,' agreed Scarne.

Suddenly a figure materialized from inside the mine. Scarne stared at him, open-mouthed, as if he had seen a ghost.

'Fernando,' he gasped.

'Is this Fernando?' demanded Manley.

'The guy who owned the mine?' asked a perplexed Leguin.

'This is Fernando. The guy I thought was dead,' Scarne confirmed.

'Lomez died, not me,' supplied Fernando. 'When we were in the mine we fought for the gun. When we were struggling the gun went off. Lomez died.'

'But what have you been doing since then?' demanded Scarne.

'Searching for gold in the mine. There's a rear entrance that I found. I've been using it for the past two years. I haven't found any gold, though.'

'How do we know that's the truth?' demanded Manley.

'You'll have to ask the Apaches. They've got a camp at the back of the mine. They've been expecting me to bring them some gold. I haven't been able to, though.'

'We still don't know whether you're telling the truth,' insisted Manley. To emphasize the point he drew his gun.

'You convinced me there was gold in the mine,' protested Scarne.

'Only because I wanted a partner to work the mine. I honestly thought there was gold there. During the last two years I've revised my opinion.'

'Look,' said Maria.

What had attracted her attention was a small group of Apaches up on the hillside. Manley aimed his revolver at them.

'Put that away,' Fernando ordered. 'They're friends.'

155

The warriors rode down the hillside. The watching group breathed a collective sigh of relief when they saw that the Apaches weren't armed.

One of them dismounted, stopped by Fernando and motioned for him to jump up on his horse. The Mexican did so.

'Wait a minute,' said Maria. She addressed the Apache in his own language.

The Apache replied. A brief conversation ensued. In the end Maria smiled. Her smile changed to laughter. The Apaches turned their horses and began to ride away. Fernando turned and gave Scarne a brief wave.

'I didn't know you spoke their language,' said Scarne.

'I learned it working in the cantina,' said Maria. 'We get some Apaches in there although they're not supposed to come in.'

'What was so funny?' demanded Manley.

'The Apache told me that yesterday they were on the point of killing Fernando since they had been feeding him for two years and he hadn't brought them a single nugget. Then the squaw whom Fernando was sleeping with said that she was pregnant. So that saved Fernando's life.'

'Did you believe him?' demanded Leguin.

'Oh, yes,' replied Maria. 'The Apaches don't tell lies. That's one white man's habit they haven't learned yet.'

*

Later that evening Maria and Scarne were in the kitchen in the cantina. Leguin and Manley were in the bar, where they commiserated with each other on not having become millionaires. Scarne thought that they both taken the news quite well. He had expected Manley to flare up at the realization, but he had merely said, 'That's that'. Leguin, too, had accepted it philosophically, saying, '*C'est la vie.*'

'What do we do next?' demanded Maria.

'We could go to Topez, as you suggested,' said Scarne.

'Yes, it's warmer there,' said Maria. 'It would be a better place to bring Juan up. I could always open a cantina.'

Scarne took off his boot.

'What are you doing,' she demanded.

He took a knife and opened up the heel. It was hollow inside. He took out a crumbled piece of paper. Maria stared in amazement as he opened the paper and produced a small yellow stone from inside.

'In fact with this you could open half a dozen cantinas,' he stated, savouring her surprise with amusement.

'Is it – gold?'

'This is real gold. Fernando gave it to me to try to persuade me that there was gold in his mine.

157

That's why I became his partner.'

Maria smiled delightedly. She came over to sit on his knee. 'Scarne, I love you,' she said.

'I think it's my gold you're after,' he replied.